The Lords of the Plains

Josiah Wakefield and his friend Dan Sturgis are buffalo hunters on the Northern Plains of Nebraska, shortly after the Civil War. Their job is to provide meat for the labourers pushing the Union Pacific Railroad relentlessly westward. Tiring of the bloody slaughter, they find work as trouble-shooters for the same railroad, as Sioux warriors are attacking the supply trains and tracklayers. However, the pair quickly discover that someone is supplying the Indians with repeating rifles, and that stolen 'Double Eagles' are the incentive.

Recovering the gold turns out to be relatively simple: keeping hold of it is something else entirely. Even the Missouri River seems to be against them. Unsure who they can trust, they return to the railhead. Here, in a familiar environment, they decide to make a stand against all comers, in the hope that they can finally bring the ringleader to account.

The Lords of the Plains

Paul Bedford

A Black Horse Western

ROBERT HALE

© Paul Bedford 2018
First published in Great Britain 2018

ISBN 978-0-7198-2712-9

The Crowood Press
The Stable Block
Crowood Lane
Ramsbury
Marlborough
Wiltshire SN8 2HR

www.bhwesterns.com

Robert Hale is an imprint
of The Crowood Press

Typeset by
Derek Doyle & Associates, Shaw Heath
Printed and bound in Great Britain by
CPI Group (UK) Ltd, Croydon, CR0 4YY

To Susan E. Peat. Many thanks for supporting my writing efforts over the years.

CHAPTER ONE

Pulling the butt tightly into my shoulder, I aimed directly at its lungs rather than going for the more obvious headshot. My choice was based on hard-earned experience. The weather had been wet for many days past; before the clouds had finally rolled on to uncover the hot sun that was now toasting my back. There would surely be hard mud caked on its bovine features. My soft lead bullet would like as not flatten out and fail to penetrate the skull. Then I would be left a mere two hundred yards away from sixteen hundred pounds of maddened beast, which was not a joyful prospect.

Satisfied that all was as well as it was ever likely to be, I eased the hammer back to full cock. The rifle boasted double-set triggers, so my retraction of the rearmost produced no noticeable result. Not so the front one! Taking a deep breath, I oh so gently caressed the slightly curved trigger. With a roar, the .52 calibre projectile sped down the thirty inch barrel and on unerringly to its target. With the cloud of black powder smoke obligingly cleared by the wind, I was able to witness the huge creature collapse to the ground. It was almost as though its legs had been retracted in unison. One moment it was munching on the verdant grass, the next it was dead. The vast body trembled uncontrollably for a few moments and then lay still.

I remained prone on the ground, a hidden sharp-shooter searching out my next target. As always, when there was no visible threat, the remaining buffalo just stood their ground, confident that their numbers would repel any assailant. That suited me just fine, because I needed a good many more kills. Only then could we roll the wagon up, butcher the cadavers and get on back to the railhead. Unlike hide hunters, I actually wanted the meat. It was what paid my way.

Retracting the hammer to 'safety and load', I eased the lever down, thereby revealing the breech. A wisp of deliciously sulphurous smoke curled up to my nostrils. Blowing into the end of the powder chamber, I reached for one of the linen cartridges placed carefully on the grass in front of me. Easing it into the breech, I then pulled the lever back up. As the rising block sealed the chamber, it also shaved off the rear of the cartridge, so exposing the black powder for ignition. Reaching into my coat pocket, I fished out a copper percussion cap. After placing the cap on the raised nipple, I squeezed firmly to ensure a tight fit. Even though I had no intention of shifting my position, old habits died hard, and throughout this process I had to make a conscious effort to stay put. Those buffalo didn't shoot back, or even wear butternut grey, but the discipline stayed with me. Satisfied that the ladder sight was correctly positioned, I levelled my trusty Sharps rifle for the next shot.

Two things then happened simultaneously: I fully cocked my weapon and the grazing buffalo moved. They moved a lot! The hairs on the back of my neck bristled, as a tremor passed through my body. Hugging the ground, I scrutinised the surrounding landscape for the cause of their alarm. The low hills surrounding my position could have easily concealed any number of threats, but something had to be visible to have spooked the herd.

Dan and Elijah were under strict instructions not to approach with the wagon until summoned. My horse was ground tethered with a purloined cavalry picket pin well to the rear. Just what was it that had got the whole herd on the move? My mouth had gone bone dry, as on every other occasion in that damned war when bloody violence had been imminent. Except this time there was no visible threat, a fact that only heightened the tension.

The buffalo were pounding off out of range, so my remaining there served no good purpose, *and* could quite possibly get me killed. Swiftly pocketing the extra cartridges, I began to crawl back towards my horse. I briefly contemplated dallying to make use of my drawtube spyglass, but then rejected the idea. It would, like as not, achieve nothing. Whoever or whatever was out there had to be close, and using the lie of the land for concealment. It was that fearful thought that persuaded me to abandon all pretence at stealth. Leaping to my feet, I ran full chisel for my mount.

As though to speed my departure, an unearthly yelp came from somewhere behind me. Was it my fevered imagination, or did it contain a note of derision? One thing was for sure: it provided wings for my flight. Without even turning, I hurtled down the gentle slope to my waiting steed. Finally reaching the animal, I yanked the pin out of the ground and literally hurled myself up into the McClellan saddle. Still clutching my fully cocked rifle, I snapped a glance back at whence I had come. What I saw was enough to chill my blood. A group of approximately twenty half-naked savages were viewing the buffalo that I had just dispatched. Then, almost as one, they all turned their baleful attention to me. That was all I needed. Tugging on the reins, I galloped pell-mell back to the wagon.

My abrupt and early return caused consternation amongst my companions. Dan Sturgis was relieving himself beside the wagon. As his head twisted round in alarm, he managed to spray his leather cavalry boots. Cursing, he called out, 'Now look what you made me do, Josiah. What in tarnation's got you in such a lather?'

Elijah, dark and taciturn, remained on the bench seat saying nothing. His way was to see much and say little.

Reining my horse in before them, I gestured along my back trail. 'If you want to mix it with a Sioux war party, stay here with your pecker in your hand. Me, I'm heading for the railhead, fast!'

In truth I didn't know whether they were Sioux or Cheyenne or even a war party, because when it came to fighting Indians I was green through and through. After the bloody actions of the previous years, both in the war and after, one would have imagined that I would be stoic in the face of danger, but as ever it was the unknown that was troubling me. All three of us had heard gory tales of the tribes out west, yet until that day none of us had actually encountered any. The mild panic that was coursing through my veins immediately infected Dan. Fair haired, bright eyed and inexhaustibly cheerful, he was, at twenty-two, the youngest of us all. Damp boots immediately forgotten, he ran to the front of the wagon and hastily clambered up on to the seat.

As the wagon was wheeled around to retrace its tracks, I looked back towards the site of my one and only kill of the day. The skyline held nothing more threatening than the occasional tree. It would be hard to justify our returning to the railhead empty-handed, but that buffalo could stay where it lay. Trotting after my companions, I felt an urge to spur my horse on to greater speed. It was Elijah that brought me down to earth. Calling over to me in a calm voice that was just loud enough to overcome the creaks and rattles of the wagon, he remarked, 'If you don't take that cannon off full cock, you'll like as not blow a hole in one of us!'

As usual we heard and saw evidence of the railhead before it actually came into view. From over the next grassy rise, a plume of black smoke ascended into the startlingly clear blue sky. As though deliberately seeking to draw our attention, a long piercing shriek announced that something quite remarkable awaited us. As we rattled over the final rise, the construction camp lay before us in all its rough-and-ready glory. Until the War betwixt the States, I had never even seen a railroad. The massive, internecine conflict rectified that, but I still never tired of gazing in awe at the mighty engines.

Modern engineering had arrived in the wilderness, and 'camp' was a misleading description. Everything was done on a vast scale, with literally hundreds of labourers employed in backbreaking work. During daylight hours nothing was static. All that mattered was forward movement. Nobody went to sleep on the same ground that they had woken on. Using sound sense, the track was being laid parallel to the existing poles of the Western Union Telegraph Company. This line had been completed some years before, and provided the benefit of near instantaneous communication with the railroad's supply base in Omaha . . . so long as neither buffalo nor Indians damaged the timber poles.

Having gratefully reached relative safety, we had

instinctively slowed our pace, so enabling me to peruse the scene before us. As usual, my eyes were drawn to the hissing steam locomotive, but it was a couple of hundred yards ahead of it where the real work was going on. Gangs of sweating men toiled incessantly, driven on by the unremitting profanity of Shaughnessy, the Irish walking boss. Iron rails thirty feet long and weighing six hundred pounds were lifted off the attendant wagons by teams of five men. They were lowered onto the waiting crossties that had been laid across ground prepared in advance by teams of graders. Then the rails were spiked down by yet more men. A measuring rod confirmed that they were always four feet eight and a half inches apart, as designated in 1863 by the now sadly deceased Abraham Lincoln. Four rails were laid each minute, hour after hour. Everything was carried out with military precision, which was not surprising, as construction of the Union Pacific was mostly in the hands of ex-officers.

Thankful though I was to have returned unscathed, my heart fell when I observed one particular individual scrutinising our progress. Thirty-seven-year-old John Stephen Casement, known as General Jack to all and sundry, had been a Brevet Brigadier General in the war and was now charged with constructing a railroad. Five feet and four inches of belligerent muscle, he was the last person that I wanted to encounter just at that moment. Unfortunately, he was the man that I had to answer to for our early return, and so reluctantly I headed directly for him. Standing square, hands on hips and beard bristling, his stance gave me no comfort.

Eyeing our empty wagon speculatively, he remarked, 'You're looking a little light, Wakefield. I don't pay you to just go sashaying around on your high horse. My men got to eat, because if they don't eat, they don't work.'

The deep voice matched his barrel chest. The accusation was clear and uncompromising. Flushed with indignation, I wanted to point out that I didn't get paid at all unless I provided meat, but it was not the time for that. Instead I replied, 'I was run off by hostiles, Mister Casement. I thought the railroad should know what's out there.'

The other man ran a meaty hand over his forehead and regarded me scornfully. 'Right now, I'm the railroad, and I don't give a shit! You see that engine, Wakefield? It only moves where there's rails laid for it to run on. I'm paid to lay those rails. No track, no dollars! This railroad is the biggest thing to hit this country, apart from that little fracas back east. No amount of dirt-worshipping heathen savages are going to stop it. Clear?'

Although reeling from his description of the War of Secession as a mere fracas, I was nevertheless about to attempt a reply. The high-pitched scream that interrupted me could have had any number of causes: a crushed toe, a severed finger or maybe a broken bone, yet somehow I knew instinctively that it wasn't any of those things. Twisting in the saddle, I was just in time

14

to witness a tracklayer stumble back and then down; an arrow shaft protruding from his chest.

The war party had approached silently, most probably shadowing our wagon. Maybe a hundred or so in number, they boiled over the rise without any discernible formation, and were upon us before we knew it. Only then, when they were in amongst us, did they start shrieking and yelling. Their hideously painted features served to emphasise a primitive savagery, the like of which few of us had encountered before.

The resultant chaos was indescribable. Even Southern irregulars could not have created such an effect. Seasoned veterans ran in any direction, leapt behind any cover; in fact did anything other than fight back. For a few vital moments, even the formidable Jack Casement seemed frozen with shock.

Leaping off my horse, I joined Dan and Elijah behind my wagon. Up and down the track swept the Godless heathens, always individually, never to command. Arrows and musket balls rained down, here and there claiming a victim. The fear that had gripped me earlier had returned, but I also found that I could still think rationally. It suddenly came to me that those wild creatures weren't attempting to *seize* the railhead. There were no reserves following on behind to exploit any initial advantage. They were there solely to create havoc, loot and kill. Hit and run! And if we did not give them a bloody nose, they would forever regard us as easy meat, much like I viewed the buffalo. With that realisation came a strange feeling of calm. It was as though I suddenly knew my enemy.

Using the wagon side as support, I levelled my rifle and retracted the hammer. Rapidly sighting down on a pair of bared shoulders, I squeezed only the foremost trigger. More pressure was required, but the short range rendered that irrelevant. With a comforting roar, the Sharps discharged and the warrior was gone, blasted forward and off his horse. My earlier emotions were now replaced by elation. Those men could be killed just like any other!

Hammer to 'safety and load'. As I retrieved another cartridge, something made me turn. Casement's intense gaze was momentarily focused solely on me. He nodded once and then was on the move, bellowing out commands as he went. Luck was definitely with him, because an arrow slammed into timber at the exact spot where he had been only seconds earlier.

My two companions had finally brought their own weapons into action and began firing at the Indians as they weaved around the camp. Elijah owned a Springfield muzzleloader, marking him out as a former infantryman, whilst Dan possessed a far more modern and potent repeating Spencer Carbine. Such a gun gave him enormous firepower, so long as he could obtain the metallic cartridges that it so greedily consumed. Working the lever action and hammer with practised speed, Dan pumped out five rounds with remarkable rapidity. Unfortunately, his enthusiasm worked against him, because not one bullet struck flesh and blood.

The discipline forged in the fires of battle gradually reasserted itself across the camp, and more gunshots crashed out from men who were now no longer easy targets. Then, as abruptly as it had begun, it was all over. The heavily outnumbered marauders sensed that it was time to withdraw. With triumphant whoops, the warriors raced away clutching hats, coats and a solitary cooking pot: the spoils of a very different kind of warfare.

As the last Indian disappeared over the brow of the hill, the men's courage returned. Taunts and exhortations began to flow freely. They had survived their first encounter with the Plains Indians. Except that not everybody had. Here and there amongst the detritus lay young men bloodily perforated by arrows. Having endured a war to make the United States of America 'is' rather than 'are', they had then come west to earn a living. Instead they had found only a cold hole in the ground.

CHAPTER TWO

As order was restored to the camp, I walked slowly over to view the victim of my marksmanship. There really wasn't much to look at. The much vaunted horse warrior was just another man like myself, except that this one had a relatively small hole in his bronzed back. I knew full well that the exit wound would be far more impressive, and so it proved. Having pulled him onto his back, I ignored the mess of blood and gore in his chest and kicked the man's thigh. It was as though I was confirming to myself that he was not invincible. As expected there was no response.

His face was concealed by long, greasy black hair. The skin tone was different to ours and his way of life certainly was, but I really didn't see anything that should have provoked the irrational fear that had apparently gripped the advancing work force, myself included. With that momentously rational thought I came to a decision.

Spinning on my heels, I called out to my two companions. 'Turn that wagon around. We're going back out there!'

Dan viewed me with genuine disbelief. His mouth tried to work, but the words would not come. Elijah, as ever, had retained some composure. 'You must have a death wish, Joe Wakefield. To go out there with those drunk fellas on the loose. Haven't you seen enough killing this day?'

The strange calmness that had come over me a short while earlier had remained, and I was suddenly very determined. 'There's a dead buffalo out there that needs skinning and butchering. I ain't leaving it for no dirt-worshippers. I shot it, which makes it mine, and I aim to get paid for it. Cartridges cost money!'

Dan had finally found his voice. 'That's just plain madness, Josiah. There's a whole war party on the loose out there. Hell, you seen what they just done.' He came from a devout Christian family, and so never shortened my first name.

'We won't have anything to fear from them. They'll be having a celebray someplace, or mourning the death of that man I just killed.' I stated that as though it was a proven fact, when in truth I had absolutely no idea what the savages might be doing.

Neither man was for turning though, but they reacted to my entreaties in different ways. Good-natured, easygoing Dan had the finer feelings that allowed for embarrassment. We had come together well before the surrender, and soon became fast friends. He had backed me up in a number of conflicts, and yet he had always been a follower to my leader. Or at least he had appeared so up until that moment.

Elijah was an altogether different case. He had only joined us a few weeks earlier in Omaha, in response to notices that I had posted around the city's dance halls and dives. He had so far proved to be capable and hardworking, yet I had not really got to know him that well. He carried with him a guarded reserve that covered him like a cloak.

In the face of their obdurate refusal, irrational anger began to build within me. I had hired them, so I could fire them! 'Very well, I'll go out alone,' I exclaimed. 'And when I get back I'll get me some more help. You two are finished around here.'

'You got no call to talk to us that way, Josiah,' protested Dan, a hurt look etched across his homely features. 'You an' me have been through a lot together. That ought to count for something.'

He was quite possibly right, but my blood was up. Some strange transformation had taken place within me. They were either with me or against me. Rigidly set on my course of action, I clambered up onto the wagon's bench seat. Taking up the reins, I was about to move off when Elijah took hold of the nearest bridle. There was a tight look to his dark features that I hadn't seen before. 'Just hold on there, Joe. Like as not you'll end up crow bait out there, and we've got spondulix coming to us. So you ain't going no place until you've settled up.'

Anger flared up within me. 'I ain't denying that, but you know how it is. All my money's tied up in this outfit. You knew that when you hired on. Hell, you've got me to thank for bankrolling this and giving you jobs.' With a conscious effort, I softened my tone, and added, 'We just need a good killing season, is all.'

Dan, standing off to one side, now looked puzzled by the sudden tension in the air. 'Surely we can wait awhile, Elijah. He'll pay us when he can. Won't you, Josiah?'

I chose to remain silent, my gaze fixed on the hard-eyed figure before me. Bizarrely, considering that we had supposedly started the day on good terms, I was now grimly weighing up my chances if Elijah should attempt to pop a cap on me. Unlike the majority of tracklayers, we both toted handguns. Our work took us way beyond the railhead, where self-reliance and a big stick counted for much.

Sitting up on the wagon, I had a height advantage but less freedom of movement. My Colt Navy Six was fully charged, but the military flap holster made little allowance for swift action. Elijah favoured the heavier calibre Colt Army but, apparently unable to afford any kind of holster, carried it tucked into his belt in the small of his back. It really was impossible to discern which of us had a clear dominance. Had we both been liquored up, with our senses dulled, it might have been a different matter. So, short of throwing stones, there was little for us to do other than glare at each other.

Such nonsense finally ended when Dan stepped between us. His fresh features carried an unusually determined look.

'I ain't about to let you two get to fighting over a few greenbacks. Josiah, if you're so all fired set on going out there, get! It just seems a pure shame, is all, because the Sioux will probably gut you before you even reach that goddamned buffalo.'

With great reluctance, Elijah finally released his hold on the bridle. Seizing my chance, I shook the reins and urged the team forward. Ahead of me, the unknown beckoned. By nightfall I might well be a naked, mutilated corpse, my bloody scalp decorating some savage's lance. *And yet*, I had signed on to provide food for the work gangs, so that was exactly what I was going to do.

As I rattled and bounced my way out onto the plains, the sounds of normality returned to the rail-head. The walking boss bellowed his relentless demands, and hammers crashed down onto rail spikes. Death may have visited the camp, but nothing was allowed to halt the inexorable advance of the Iron Horse.

It was as though I was wallowing in a sea of blood. The sticky liquid dripped from every finger, coated every surface. A warm wind rustled the long grass around me, but other than that the only audible sound was the noise of my own exertions. Initially, the fear of discovery had held me in its grip, but that sensation had soon been overwhelmed by other even more visceral emotions. I felt sick to my gut at the ghastly sight before me, and yet my task was far from over. The great oozing beast would provide enough meat for many hungry men, but the removal of it was no easy task.

Having run my knife down the line of its spine from neck to croup, I had then flayed the hide down to the belly on both sides. I had seen this done many times before by my erstwhile employees, but always from a distance. My elevated role had been to kill the creatures, and then keep lookout for any unwelcome visitors. I purchased the expensive ammunition, so I sure as hell didn't have to butcher the victims of it as well.

My flesh crawled as I stripped out the two long bands of fat lying along either side of the spine. Could the camp cooks really use that? Practicality overcame revulsion. I threw the nauseating blubber onto the flat bed of the wagon. This unpleasantly close encounter was beginning to make me wonder how Dan and Elijah could do such revolting work day after day.

The hump and ribs were the favoured red-meat cuts. I sliced into those with a feverish urgency. Time was passing. To be alone on the suddenly menacing plains in darkness, with only a slow moving wagon for transport was a fearsome prospect. Sweat streamed profusely down my blood-spattered face as I separated the prime tissue from the offal. Whether sheer dread or exertion was the cause was irrelevant. I was not leaving that desolate spot until my task was finished.

Finally, the last of the huge bloody steaks had been heaved aboard. I cast a long, apprehensive look around me. The ever-present wind was my only companion on that bleak landscape. Quite possibly the war party was indeed having a celebration, secure in the knowledge that their camp was safe from retribution. They certainly could not have expected a lone, foolhardy individual to return to the scene of a single buffalo kill.

Gratefully I wiped my gory hands on the thick grass. My eyes were drawn to the huge skull gazing reproachfully at me. I recalled that its tongue was considered to be a great delicacy. Well, the connoisseurs would just have to do without. I had had more than my fill of hacking and cutting for one day. Indeed, for many a day. It occurred to me that I would either have to find some new skinners fast, or get into another line of work. There was no way that I could have known just how prescient that realisation was!

CHAPTER THREE

The new day arrived in the same fashion, although never the same location, as did every other one at the railhead. I was dragged out of a deep sleep by the foul-mouthed demands of the walking boss. Around me in the huge, but densely packed railroad car, nearly two hundred men assigned to bunks three tiers high suffered the same fate. A full breakfast awaited them and then, rain or shine, hot or cold, the relentless activity commenced. Any man, in any army, would have immediately recognized the regime.

Theoretically I could have dallied in my bunk, thereby emphasising my differing status. But what would have been the point? I was wide-awake, so such gratuitous behaviour would have merely provoked resentment, and served no good purpose. The only men immune to any criticism were the night guards, detailed as a direct result of the raid, who collapsed onto still warm blankets without a word. Had they been minded, they might have pointed out just how toxically flatulent the atmosphere had become during the night. Men who ate well, rarely bathed and almost never washed their clothes, became immune to the myriad vapours that they produced.

Outside, the beginnings of a pleasant spring day awaited me. Kicking on my boots, I dropped down from the rail car. Splashing my face with water from a tin basin, I suddenly recalled the previous days events. 'Hey boys,' I announced to anyone that might be listening, 'we're all Indian fighters now!'

That remark was greeted by hoots of well-meaning derision. 'Sure, and you're a fine man, Josiah Wakefield, with your big Sharps rifle. You'll be after saving us all from dem heathens!'

The funning was good-natured; the accent serving to remind anyone who cared that so many of the men hailed from the Emerald Isle. It also highlighted the fact that the men had hired on to lay track, not fight savages. Which, of course, was exactly what I might have to do again that day, *if* I rattled out onto the prairie. We only got paid when we produced meat for the workforce, which meant venturing out well away from the railhead to find the nearest buffalo herd. *We!* Ha, a fine trick of the mind. It wasn't 'we' anymore, not after the previous day's petulant display. I had effectively dismissed my workforce. And yet they weren't just employees. Dan had also been a good friend.

Now in a far more sombre mood, I clambered back into the railroad car to recover my weapons. After the events of the previous day, I had vowed to keep them with me at all times, which included the rowdy 'free-for-all' breakfast supplied by the Union Pacific. Any residual good cheer effectively vanished when I failed to see either of my skinners. How on earth was I going to fulfil my contract with the railroad? At best it would require an unwelcome trip to Omaha to recruit more men, with a consequent loss of earnings.

Such glum thoughts were still exercising my mind, when shortly after I spied the stocky figure of Jack Casement, approaching me at a fast pace. That was in itself strange. If a man in his exalted position wanted someone, he sent for him. It was also unusual to observe him in a formal coat. Most times he settled for a rough woollen jacket or just shirtsleeves. As he ground to a halt before me, the former general eyed the rifle in my right hand and smiled slightly, as though I had just confirmed something for him. Turning slightly he gestured back towards the finely painted railway car from which he had emanated. Two men wearing sober, but obviously expensive frock coats were in deep discussion on the open platform at the end of the carriage. Without preamble, Casement demanded, 'You see the one on the right?'

'I do.'

'That there is Grenville Mellen Dodge. As chief engineer, he is in charge of the whole shooting match. I might be your boss, but he is God. So that's "Mister Dodge" to you, or "General" or just plain "Sir".'

'Why?' I replied somewhat cockily. 'I ain't in the

army any more, nor subject to its regulations. In fact I ain't subject to *anything* that I can rightly think on.'

Scratching his plentiful beard, Casement eyed me pityingly. 'Excepting maybe the need to scratch a living,' he replied, and then abruptly stepped so close to me that I could almost *taste* the odour of cigars that habitually clung to him. Reaching up, he placed a great paw on my left shoulder. I considered myself to be well formed, and sound of limb and lung, but the unexpected pressure was breathtaking. What he lacked in height, her certainly made up for in raw power. It was rumoured that he had once single-handedly lifted a thirty feet long, six hundred pound rail off the ground, and suddenly I fully believed it. Unable to move had I even wanted to, I now found myself transfixed by his piercing blue eyes.

'You're like all the other young fellas around here. You came out of the army with barely a dime to your name, but because you've seen something of the world, you think you're beholden to none. Having said all that, you were the only man to bring down one of those hostiles yesterday, and I heard about you heading back out there to recover that meat. That took grit.' He paused for a moment, as though unused to handing out compliments, before recalling that he was there for a higher purpose. 'You got something, Wakefield, and General Dodge wants to use it. And what he wants, he gets. So you mind your manners around him, or I'll smash you flatter than hammered shit!' With that, he suddenly released his grip, placed

a horny hand between my shoulder blades and pro-
pelled me none too gently towards the ornate
carriage.

The two men had walked back in, and it was obviously intended that I should follow. In truth, I was
actually a little nervous. Everyone knew of General
Dodge. As well as being a capable soldier, he was also
an acknowledged expert on railroads, and during the
war had been given control of them by none other
than Ulysses S. Grant. Now he was a man on a mission,
and that was to push the Union Pacific on across the
vast empty expanse of the northern plains until it
linked up with the Central Pacific heading east. The
only problem was that the plains were not *completely*
empty!

As I entered the highly polished interior, I found
the railroad boss waiting for me behind an expansive
desk. His companion and only other occupant of the
carriage sat off to one side, eyes focused resolutely on
the floor. This individual was obviously small of
stature, and sported a pencil thin moustache. His
frockcoat was well tailored and immaculately brushed,
and the leather shoes polished to an unbelievable
shine. The overall appearance bespoke of a great deal
of money, and one thing was for sure: whatever his
role in life was, it certainly didn't involve any manual
labour or indeed me, and so I directed my attention
elsewhere.

The chief engineer was a man of lean build, with a
neatly cut beard who immediately settled his eyes on

mine. They were penetrating, but not unkind, and I recalled hearing that he was reputed to be a basically decent man driven by great ambition. Then again, hearsay was often wrong, and without deigning to offer me a chair, Dodge got straight to the point.

'Mister Casement informs me that you are an accomplished Indian fighter and that you possess grit. Well, if you're to work for me, you'll need it.'

'I thought I was already working for you,' I replied obtusely.

Casement gave a derisive snort, but Dodge continued as though I had not even spoken. 'If we are ever going to claim what we bought from the French, we need to build this railroad. Yesterday's events confirmed yet again what Lewis and Clark discovered sixty years ago. The Sioux are definitely hostile, and so I need men to fight them.'

I stared at the chief engineer in astonishment, before cobbling together an answer of sorts. 'I shot my first and only Indian yesterday, in self-defence, because they attacked us.'

Dodge waved away such specifics. 'That's more than most of us have done out here, which makes you the right man in the right place. That was not the first hit and run attack that we've suffered. Far from it. They've been striking at surveyors and graders, and supply wagons. Those damned heathens sweep in out of nowhere, cause havoc and then disappear. They even stole a payroll strongbox from one wagon, filled with gold Double Eagles, although God alone knows what use they'd find for so much specie. General Sherman has promised me army protection, but we may have to wait awhile. With the war over, the country's forces are shrinking rapidly, and a sizeable chunk of what's left is required in the South for reconstruction. So in the meantime, the Union Pacific needs someone like you watching its flank. Mister Casement admits to learning a lesson yesterday, and certainly won't ignore any more of your warnings. Any news of importance can be relayed to me by telegraph.'

I was taken aback by what seemed to be a new job offer, but was also more than a little dubious. 'If I *was* to do that, then I'd need someone watching *my* back. I ain't going out there all on my lonesome.'

Casement was ready with the answer to that. 'Don't see that as a problem. That fresh-faced skinner you employed is still in camp.'

Although happily surprised at that revelation, one more problem occurred to me. 'Who'll do my job? Your men will still need feeding.'

The burly track boss had an answer for that as well. 'Don't you concern yourself, Wakefield. Just so happens that a new outfit pulled in last night, while you were out on the cold, hard prairie on your lonesome. It's led by some young fella, name of Bill Cody. Cocky son of a bitch . . . a bit like you. Says he's a real sure shot. Happen you'll meet him afore long. You might even rub shoulders out there somewhere.'

'Can't wait,' I remarked with a noticeable lack of

31

enthusiasm. It hadn't escaped my notice that nobody had mentioned money, but that was about to change.

'You'll get ten dollars a day, and found,' Dodge announced, 'and five dollars and found for every man you hire. Get out there and be our eyes and ears. Oh, and a word to the wise, Mister Wakefield: cut the flap off that holster. The extra speed might just save your life one day. Good day to you.' And with that the interview was over abruptly. He turned towards the other man, who had appeared strangely disinterested throughout the interview, and left Casement to usher me out of the carriage. It was also left to the track boss to supply the nitty gritty.

'You can draw all the powder and ball that you need gratis from now on, and move your possibles in with the walking boss when you're in camp . . . which won't be often. The general expects results, so you'd better get to it.' And so saying, he too turned away, leaving me alone with a new job and little idea of how to tackle it.

Ten dollars a day and found, plus unlimited ammunition! That was damned good money. The average track hand earned only two dollars and fifty cents *and* had to pay for room and board. Such potential riches should have filled me with good cheer, but there was a tight feeling in my gut as I searched for Dan. There would be no choice other than for me to eat humble pie. Yet as it turned out, our reconciliation was easier than I had expected. Approaching my team, I spotted his fresh-faced figure lounging by the wagon. On seeing me draw near, he shifted uncomfortably before making eye contact.

'Thought you might have lit out on me,' I remarked.

'Nah. We got through that damned war, so I ain't splitting now. But you said some powerful harsh words yesterday, Josiah. There was no call to get all wrathy. I ain't ever fought Indians before, and the thought of going back out there kind of unmanned me.' This was uttered apologetically. Dan was plainly seeking to rebuild bridges, and now of all times I had no reason to push him away.

Quickly thrusting out my right hand, I stated, 'Reckon I could have been a mite hasty. Let's just let bygones be bygones.' Moving on quickly, I enquired, 'Where's Elijah, anyhu?'

Accepting my grip with obvious relief, Dan muttered, 'Gone!'

'Gone where?'

'Just up and took off. Probably hitched a lift on the train returning to Omaha for supplies. You'd best watch yourself if you and him ever meet up again. He seemed like a dark one.'

Shrugging off that development, I related the content of my meeting with the chief engineer, and then quickly followed on by offering Dan another job at better money. Although, since we were to be effectively a partnership, I thought it prudent not to mention my own remuneration.

His youthful face lit up with delight. 'Five dollars a day!' he exclaimed.

'And found,' I added. 'Plus cartridges. *And* you won't be wallowing in blood everyday either.'

At the mention of blood, Dan's features clouded over. 'It occurs to me that hunting Indians sounds a whole heap more dangerous. How do you propose to go about it, anyhu?'

That was a good question, because although I'd served as a skirmisher with Colonel Hiram Berdan's Sharpshooters in the war, I'd never fought any of the wild tribes before. 'Well, I guess we just need to go looking,' I finally managed. What we would do if we found something was another thing altogether.

It was later on that same morning when the two of us set out on our new mission. This time we were travelling light. No wagon, or even a pack mule; just what we could carry in our bulging saddlebags. My own, now redundant, wagon and team had been left in the care of the railhead farrier. He had instructions to sell them, but only if a good price could be obtained.

I had refined my vague plans somewhat. Since the Sioux undoubtedly knew where the railroad was, it made sense for us to attempt to discover the location of their camp. Because, as my pa had never tired of saying, 'knowledge is power'.

To hopefully mislead anyone that might be watching,

we initially set off to the north, before sweeping around in a wide semi-circle out of sight of the railhead. Then we deliberately made for the site of the buffalo that I had reluctantly butchered. In the absence of any definite strategy, it seemed like as good a place to begin as any.

As we approached the remains of the great beast, with its head still untouched by carrion, I had the irrational thought that its sightless eyes were regarding me reproachfully.

Dan had a far more practical turn of mind. 'Did you think to cut out its tongue?' he enquired eagerly.

I sighed. 'No. No, I didn't. But don't let that stop you.'

It didn't. Gleefully dismounting, Dan drew his knife and moved in, recklessly oblivious to his wider surroundings. It was left to me to keep watch. Kneeling down in front of the ruined creature, he struggled for a considerable time to prize open its jaws. However, once inside, it then took only moments to slice out the long thick tongue. His only recently relinquished line of work meant that he had displayed no signs of squeamishness whatsoever.

'You must want that thing really bad,' I remarked doubtfully, all the while searching the surrounding terrain for any sign of hostiles.

He shook his head in amazement. 'I can't believe you've never eaten one of these. I've heard of folks killing these poor beasts for the tongue alone. Boil it up, and you get a delicious fatty meal. It's no wonder they fetch good money. If you're lucky, I might just let you try some.'

'Yeah, yeah,' I muttered ungraciously. I was on edge, and wanted nothing more than to get moving again. Having got well clear of the Iron Horse, the only sound was that of the wind rustling the long grass, which stretched away seemingly endlessly in all directions. And now that I was no longer hunting dumb animals, I found the relative silence strangely unnerving, but knew that I would just have to get used to it if I was to succeed in my new role.

Dan wrapped the severed meat in some cloth and stuffed it into a pocket. It was obvious that he fully intended eating it before the day was out. Only then, with business finally concluded, did he suddenly appear to sense my disquiet. 'Which direction did the Sioux come from when you first saw them?'

'I've no idea,' I responded unhelpfully. 'The herd saw them first, and then that spooked me.' Sighing, I added, 'I reckon we should keep heading south for a while, at least for today, and then turn west. Shit, this is like stalking a grizzly without having any idea where it is!'

My companion frowned. The magnitude of what we had undertaken was beginning to sink in. 'But what if we. . . ?'

As though by divine timing, a single muted gunshot rang out. Although distant and barely audible, for me there could be no doubting its identity. 'If that ain't a

Sharps, I'm a horned toad!'

The two of us waited in expectant silence until, some moments later, the sound was repeated. And this time we could definitely discern that it came from the west of us.

'You know what I reckon?' Dan ventured. 'I think it's that new hunting outfit you told me about. I believe I saw one of them strutting about in buckskins, while you was jawing with the quality in that fancy carriage. If they're all the way out here by now, then they're keen, I'll give them that.'

As an idea came to me, I nodded slowly. 'And, we might not be the only ones to hear that shooting. Let's go take a look see, but for Christ's sake keep your eyes peeled, unless you want to end up like a pin cushion!'

By the time that we got within sight, two more shots had crashed out, each one louder than the last. Then there had been only the sound of the wind and our horses. Perhaps he'd shot his fill for the day. Anxious not to blunder into anything, I reined in and extended my drawtube spyglass. It was as I had thought.

'He's done with killing,' I reported. 'Looks like there's ten of the big shaggies to carve up, and the wagon's joining him with the skinners.'

'Anyone on it we know?' Dan queried, pointedly. He obviously hadn't completely dismissed Elijah from his thoughts, as I had.

'Too far off to make out the faces,' I replied. 'This

37

thing ain't magic, you know, and it's had its fair share of knocks.'

'Aw shit!' my friend exclaimed abruptly. 'I bet it can make out those devils, though!'

CHAPTER FOUR

Swinging around in alarm, I followed the line of his outstretched hand. I sure as hell didn't need any lenses this time. Off to the south, concealed behind a low rise, of which there seemed to be so many on the plains, was a Sioux war party. They numbered about thirty and, oblivious to our arrival, were apparently about to charge the buffalo hunters. Swiftly dismounting, I ground tethered my animal and drew the Sharps out of its scabbard.

'You right sure about this, Josiah?' Dan asked nervously. 'I mean, we could just slip away and no one would know.' Even as he uttered that, he was colouring with embarrassment, because he well knew that such a suggestion wasn't really worthy of him.

'*We'd know*!' I snapped back. 'And this time make your shots count. Don't just blast away like you're having a conniption fit.' I knew that I was being overly harsh, but my own nerves were stretched taut . . . and the situation was only going to get worse. Before contracting the spyglass, I took a closer look at the war party. What I saw momentarily took my breath away. 'Sweet Jesus! Some of those savages are carrying Henry repeaters.'

Alarm flashed across Dan's youthful features. 'Are you sure? How can that be? Even the army doesn't have those.'

Snapping the glass shut, I retorted, 'We'll have to be mighty careful here. We'll let the Sioux attack the hunters, and then hit them from behind. Surprise should give us an edge, especially if they don't know how many of us there are.'

Dan regarded me solemnly, but to his credit this time he didn't quibble. He just took hold of his own long gun and silently retracted the hammer. The two of us stood side by side, gauging the distance, when quite suddenly the war party burst into action. Rapidly working their ponies up to a gallop, they careered over the rise and down towards the startled buffalo hunters. Rifles cracked out, as the warriors opened up with their repeaters.

'Wait 'til the hunters fire back,' I commanded. 'Then the Sioux won't spot us too soon . . . I hope.' As we both levelled our weapons in readiness, I quickly added, 'And aim for their ponies.' The distance was increasing all the time, and so it made sense to aim for the largest target. Putting someone afoot was likely to make him more reasonable.

As the no doubt startled white men responded with their own gunfire, I drew a fine bead on a pair of haunches and fired. With the ever-present wind blowing the powder smoke away, I witnessed the poor beast slew sideways. Its rider was hurled to the ground with great force. At my side, Dan's Spencer crashed out with comforting ferocity, and he too brought a pony and rider tumbling to earth.

We were both able to get in two more shots with mixed results, before the rearmost warriors realized that they were under attack from behind. Then the war party suddenly fragmented, and became an entity of two halves. Those in front continued to bear down on the hated buffalo hunters, whilst those at the back milled around in confusion as they tried to locate their assailants.

Dan rapidly loosed off another shot, but he rushed it and so inevitably missed. The necessity to reload my single-shot weapon meant that my pace was slower and I took a more deliberate aim. This time I struck my target broadside on, with the inevitable bloody result. Three men were now unhorsed, with another one wounded in the left shoulder, but two of them were back on their feet and all of them had finally realized where we were. The question was, what would they do about us?

If I had been in their place, I would have hunkered down, and returned rapid fire with the Henry rifles, but the Sioux were part of a horse culture that thrived on movement. Instinctively, those still mounted swung

41

their ponies around and made directly for us. As they rapidly closed the distance, we could make out strange cries that sounded like '*Hoka He.*'

It's only the stupid that never scare, and I had a pretty fair idea how my partner must be feeling, because fear was stabbing at my guts as well. 'Stand your ground, Dan,' I commanded firmly. 'Those sons of bitches won't be able to hit anything at that speed!'

And wasn't that just a fact? The approaching riders got off a few wild shots to accompany their howls, but none of the projectiles came anywhere near us. Then, as the distance dropped to around fifty yards, we both fired at two more unfortunate animals. The pair collapsed as though their forelegs had been snapped, throwing their hapless riders to the ground. Dan levered in another cartridge and shot one of the men straight through his chest, just as he vaulted to his feet. I, on the other hand, dropped my empty Sharps and drew my Colt from its now open-topped holster. Thumbing back the hammer, I fired again and again.

The supposedly ferocious attack stalled abruptly in the face of our staunch defence, and the warriors wheeled sharply off to their right. One of the dismounted survivors leapt up behind another and then the whole group fled back from whence they had originally come. Over near the hunters, the departure of half their number had severely disconcerted the front-runners of the war party. They too were coming under sustained fire, and any advantage of surprise was now completely lost. As though by mutual consent, they completely abandoned the assault. All that could were soon racing after their rearguard, slowing only to pick up one of the survivors of our first volley.

'Hot dang!' Dan yelled excitedly. 'Ain't that a sight to see? We've actually gone and run them off.'

Nodding with relief, I was gratified to observe that even through his excitement, my companion had the presence of mind to reload his Spencer. Removing the tube from the butt, he carefully slid fresh cartridges into the magazine until it contained its full quota of seven.

'Seems like we really *are* Indian fighters now, don't it?' I observed, recalling my earlier blasé comment back at the railhead. With that, I reloaded my Sharps, retrieved my horse, and moved cautiously towards the still figure lying in the long grass. I kept my weapon trained on him until I noticed that his head was resting at an impossible angle to his torso. Only then did I relax.

'Neck's broke,' I remarked to Dan, as he came up behind me. Leaning down, I recovered the Henry rifle from the long grass. It was in decent condition, and more to the point contained a full magazine. I also found some spares in a hide pouch slung over the dead man's torso. 'These sons of bitches don't seem to have any shortage of metallic cartridges. Really does make you wonder who they got them from.'

Since the bronzed corpse could tell us nothing, we both mounted up and continued on to join the hunters who were congregated around their wagon. I had at least benefited from the violent encounter, because I now owned a modern repeating rifle as well as my long-range man stopper. The other apparently dead body that we passed on the way possessed only a bow and arrows, so we didn't bother to check it over, but I did empty a .44-rimfire cartridge from my new acquisition into its skull . . . just to be on the safe side! The Henry's lever action proved to be extremely smooth and satisfying to operate.

Three of the waiting men regarded us with interest, as we walked our horses up to their wagon. The fourth was in too much pain to pay us any mind. He was nursing his blood-soaked left arm, which had a rudimentary bandage tied around it. I experienced a vague sense of relief on discovering that Elijah was not a member of the new outfit.

One individual immediately stood out from the rest, and not just because of the Sharps rifle cradled in his left arm. Of medium height, and clad in a mountain man's buckskins, he appeared to be barely out of his teens, but his eyes blazed with wit and intelligence. A sweat-stained slouch hat was worn at a jaunty angle, indicating that appearance played as much a part as practicality. Underneath a wispy moustache, a smile played on his lips, although whether that was out of amusement or welcome we had yet to find out. My immediate, instinctive assessment was that he was likely to be short on experience, but big on bravado.

'Mighty fortunate for you fellas that we happened along,' the young man brayed loudly.

'You must be Cody,' I remarked somewhat stiffly, deciding that I had apparently summed him up correctly. 'Mister Casement said that you might be out here somewhere.'

' "Bill" to my friends,' he threw back. 'And if I kill enough of these big dumb beasts, I think I'll stick "Buffalo" in front of it. Has a nice ring to it, don't it?'

'It might do if you live that long,' Dan retorted angrily. 'As it is, you seem to have a very hare-brained view of things. But for us, those cockchafers would have claimed your scalps!'

Cody bristled at the accusing tone. 'That's some tongue you got on you, Mister,' came his sharp rejoinder.

'Well, yeah, actually it is.' So saying, and with a decidedly music hall flourish, Dan produced the severed buffalo tongue from his pocket. 'And it's all mine!'

For a long moment there was complete silence, and then the young buffalo hunter slapped his thigh . . . hard. 'Haw, haw, haw,' he guffawed loudly. 'You boys are all right!'

That was followed by another long silence, as we all gazed at each other, as young men do when they're sizing each other up. Then, realizing that we were after all on the same side, I resolved to work with what we had and make the best of the situation. 'I'm Joe

Wakefield and the man with the nourishing meal is Dan Sturgis. As you've probably realized we work for the Union Pacific, just like you, only we don't hunt big shaggies any more.

Cody raised his eyebrows. 'Ah, so we've got you to thank for us getting a job so quickly.' Then he fell silent again and waited. It was very noticeable that he hadn't *actually* thanked us.

'Yes, you could say that,' I pointedly replied. 'And now we need you to do something for us in return.'

The other man smiled brightly, undeterred by a sudden loud groan from his wounded companion. 'Well, hell, Joe. Of course I will. We're all friends together, now, ain't we?'

'When you get back to the railhead, I'd be obliged if you'd tell Casement everything that occurred here. Tell him we're following the band that attacked you. And what's really important is that you mention this.' Brandishing the Henry rifle, I continued with, 'Some bastards are selling these to the Sioux. If the Indians get enough of them, his railroad could be in real trouble.'

Cody viewed the gleaming weapon with hungry eyes. 'What say you give me that, so I can show it to him?'

Despite the warmth in the air, I could feel a chill settle over me. 'Nah, happen not. I killed a man for this gun, so I reckon I'll hang on to it.'

'Just as you like,' he replied, his disappointment obvious. 'But you can rely on me. I'll be sure and tell him everything.'

The wounded skinner moaned even more loudly, and I glanced at his boss enquiringly. 'He sounds in a bad way. Anything we can do to help?'

'Nah, he'll be right,' came the dismissive reply. 'Bullet went straight through the fleshy part of his arm. It's nought but a scratch. The sawbones at the railhead'll fix him up, and he'll be back working tomorrow.'

From the amount of blood coating the bandage, it looked far more than any scratch, but I'd suddenly had enough of this loudmouth and was keen to be off. 'You be sure to tell Casement *exactly* what occurred,' I urged Cody insistently. 'It's important that he knows we're doing our job out here.'

The buckskinned figure laughed just a little too long and a little too loud for my taste. 'Don't you trouble yourself, Joe. I won't go stealing your glory.' With that, he turned to his men, none of whom had so far uttered a word, and remarked, 'You got plenty of cutting up to do, boys. You don't want to be here come nightfall, 'cause we won't have Mister Wakefield to protect us!'

Dan waited until we were well out of sight, before putting the question. 'You think he'll tell Casement *exactly* how it happened?'

I didn't have to give that any thought at all. 'I think he'll tell him *exactly* what suits *Buffalo* Bill. That's what I think. The man's a glory hunter, just like some of those generals in the war. I remember a fella, name of Custer, with his long curls and fancy uniforms. What a blowhard he was!'

'So why don't we go back to the railhead as well?' Dan asked with obvious eagerness.

'Because there's a mighty fresh trail to follow over yonder. If we can find out where their camp is, we'll have a hell of a lot more to tell the track boss. *And* it would be very useful if we could find out who is supplying these rifles to the Sioux.'

'OK, OK,' Dan reluctantly agreed. 'But I'm powerful hungry, and this tongue's weighing heavy on me. Let's stop soon and cook it, 'cause there's no way we want to be showing firelight once darkness falls.'

There was plenty of sense in that, and in truth I was hungry, too, but first I wanted to cover some more distance. I knew that if we kept heading south, we would eventually reach the Little Blue River. Somewhere along its course I hoped to find the Indian encampment . . . without getting too close to it. Failing that, the next river of any size was the Republican, but that was almost into Kansas and would take us much too far from the railhead. After all, our job was also to act as lookout and forewarn of any raiding parties threatening the Union Pacific. We sure as hell couldn't do that if we weren't even in Nebraska Territory.

The keenly anticipated buffalo tongue, boiled to perfection over a small fire, had tasted every bit as good as Dan had promised. He had very generously shared it with me, and after supplementing it with a plentiful helping of the frontier staple of beans we had both eaten our fill. A piping hot mug of coffee apiece had rounded off a perfect meal, and we welcomed the prospect of a good night's shuteye. With darkness falling, I kicked out the fire and laid out my bedroll. Of necessity it was to be a cold camp, but that would be no hardship in such mild conditions.

Dan peered at me curiously in the gathering gloom. 'Just what are your intentions if we find this Sioux camp? My ma didn't raise me just to end up staked out on the prairie with my pecker in my mouth, you know. I've heard the nightmare stories about these heathens, just like you have.'

I sighed. 'Don't it ever occur to you that they might have good reason to hate us? They were here first, you know.' I paused to see if he would comment on that, but he didn't choose to. 'Well, anyhu, I figure that once we find them, *if* we find them, we hightail it back to the railhead. I'm no hero, and we'll have done what we've been paid to. My spyglass should help me to see how many are toting repeaters. After that, it'll be up to General Dodge as to . . .' The faintest of sounds registered with me and I froze.

Dan made to start speaking, but I waved him to silence. Straining to hear, I could *just* make out something that wasn't the wind. Thankfully the darkness was now almost complete, because whatever was out there seemed to be coming our way. I just prayed that there weren't any residual cooking smells in the air.

Then gradually I began to make out the rattling of moving parts. That could only indicate a wagon. But who the hell would be travelling with one across the plains during the night?

'See to your horse,' I hissed at my companion.

The last thing we needed was to be given away by our own animals. Nothing was visible through the murk, but there could be no mistaking the fact that the vehicle appeared to be moving directly towards us.

'Christ!' I muttered half to myself. 'Out of the whole northern plains, they have to pick this spot.' Yet even as I spoke, a possible reason occurred to me, and for the second time in as many days an unpleasant chill settled on me. I contemplated drawing my revolver, but decided against it. The last thing I wanted was another fight on my hands. Far better to just let them go about their business.

The creaking and clatter got louder and louder, until I was convinced that the unidentified newcomers must surely blunder into us. To my overburdened senses, the great heft of the wagon and its contents was almost palpable. Although gently stroking my animal's forehead, I nevertheless kept an iron grip on its muzzle. Somehow feeling my disquiet, it shifted restlessly. And then, like ships in the night, they were past us without either side even seeing each other. As the noise began to recede, I distinctly heard a harsh voice proclaim, 'Those goddamn savages had better not have moved camp!'

If he received a reply to that, I did not hear it, but

the implications were breathtaking and confirmed my earlier notion. As the sounds of the heavy vehicle gradually dissipated, I came to a snap decision. 'Pack up your possibles,' I ordered softly. 'We're gonna follow those sons of bitches. They obviously know where they're going, which is certainly more than we do!'

Dan was aghast. 'But we don't even know who they are. They could lead us clean down to Mexico!'

It was true that I was acting on a hunch, but something told me that it was a sure bet. 'It *can't* be a coincidence that they just happen to be travelling in the same direction as both us *and* that war party. Which suggests to me that they're intending to do a little trading with the Sioux, and ain't it a fact that those same fellas have suddenly come into better weapons than you're toting?'

The logic of my argument was undeniable, even though my young friend would quite obviously rather be wrapped up in his bedroll. But then for that matter, so would I, except that, as ever, something was pushing me that bit harder than my more laid-back companion. Which was probably why I was the one earning ten dollars a day!

With the bedrolls and cooking utensils packed away we were ready to be off, but this would be far from any kind of chase. Once back in earshot of the rattling conveyance, we would be following on foot. That would be fast enough to keep pace with the mysterious strangers, without risking injury to our mounts. And so once again we set off into the unknown, only this time we knew for a fact that we weren't alone. It was also true that we could well be about to enter a world of hurt!

CHAPTER FIVE

'Sweet Jesus! Will you look at that lot?' exclaimed Dan with a mixture of fear and amazement.

The two of us were belly down in the long grass, gazing in astonishment at the huge native encampment stretching out before our very eyes. Scores and scores of tipis were situated along the northern bank of the Little Blue River. The hide coverings were colourfully daubed with various unintelligible symbols. A huge extended pony herd grazed in the lush grass growing by the side of the sparkling watercourse. Conveniently nearby was a large stand of trees, providing fuel for heat and light. It was quite obvious that the well-chosen and stunningly scenic location provided perfectly for all the Sioux's basic needs. Far from any white settlements, they appeared to feel totally secure, because there were no visible sentries, and only a few mangy dogs available to raise the alarm.

It was well after first light, and so wisps of smoke drifted up from many cooking fires. A strong instinct for self-preservation meant that the wagon's occupants had waited until the camp was up and about before rolling into view. There were three of them, and at first glance all were strangers to me, although the distance was too great for me to discern their features accurately. Now, as they unloaded a variety of wooden crates to the ground, they seemed to be the centre of attention for every warrior and child of the tribe.

'We've struck pay dirt here, all right,' I responded quietly.

In truth I was stunned by the overall magnitude of our discovery. Extending my drawtube spyglass, I settled it on the merchandise that we had been following throughout the night. As the white men levered open a couple of crates, it was obvious that they weren't there to trade blankets, beads and cooking pots. Their stock was of a far more lethal nature. From one box came a Henry rifle, and from the other a jug that could only have contained strong liquor. These traders were very obviously looking to get rich on other people's misery!

It was soon apparent that Dan Sturgis felt that he had seen enough. 'Right. Well that's that then,' he whispered in my ear. 'This is the pot of gold at the end of the rainbow. With news like this, we should be good for a bonus. Let's make tracks while they're all busy.'

The only problem with that suggestion was that an idea of pure madness had just swept over me. Keeping my head down, I turned to my friend. 'Don't it make you wonder just how those traders were able to travel here in safety?'

A sick look came into Dan's eyes. He should have known it wasn't going to be that easy. 'Well, obviously they have things that the Sioux want,' he ventured.

'Yeah, but how did they make first contact without having their scalps lifted? You've seen what happens whenever those Indians encounter a white man.'

With a visibly sinking heart, my companion replied quietly, 'I don't know the answer to that.'

'Neither do I,' I retorted. 'But I'm damn well going to find out!'

Dan groaned. 'I knew I should have asked Cody for a job. Thinking on that wound, I'd say he's gonna be a man short for a while.'

I favoured him with what I hoped was a winsome smile, and patted his right forearm. 'You'd be lost without me . . . and I without you. Besides, you'd soon have tired of that Cody's big mouth, and butchering critters is an awful job. I know. I tried it.'

'All right, all right, I'm with you! Just don't go all mushy on me.' He paused before emitting a deep sigh. 'I suppose you've got a plan. You always seem to.'

He'd wrong-footed me with that one, because I hadn't actually considered how we were going to proceed. And yet, thinking about it, there wasn't really a great deal to chew over.

'It's a pretty simple one, I guess. Once they're well clear of that camp, we jump them, and try to take at least one alive.' Something specific had occurred to me though. 'One thing: we'll have to keep watch on them until they leave, 'cause we don't really know where they've come from, and we certainly don't know where they're going.' Deep down, I knew that achieving all that would be a great deal harder than saying it!

It was noon the following day before the traders finally bid their farewells. They had obviously been benefiting from tribal hospitality, whereas our long vigil had been far less pleasant. Even though stationed well back from the encampment, we had needed to be constantly on the alert for any travellers, especially during the daylight hours. At night, we had managed to sleep fitfully, sharing the watch keeping equally. Food had been a mixture of beef jerky and pemmican, washed down with water from our canteens. Now, at last, it appeared that our waiting was over, and that we were to discover which direction the traders would take.

For some time they had been loading up the wagon with vast numbers of animal hides, and a variety of strange looking blocks, the composition of which completely baffled me. The final object to be handed up definitely made me blink with surprise, especially as it took two men to do it. Even seen through indifferent lenses at great distance, there could be no mistaking a metal-bound strongbox!

Glancing at my companion, I muttered, 'They just loaded a strongbox into the wagon.'

Dan peered at me incredulously. 'What the hell would Indians be doing with a strongbox?'

'Well, I recall Dodge saying that one had been carried off in a raid,' I replied. 'If you ask me, this is all getting pretty murky! It's almost as though . . .'

My speech abruptly ceased, as the wagon, drawn by a team of four oxen, pulled out of the Sioux encampment moving east and following the course of the river. Its heading momentarily gave me pause, until suddenly the penny dropped. 'Of course!' I exclaimed. 'They're making for the Missouri River. Once there, they've got paddle steamers to take them anywhere.'

'Unless we stop them first,' Dan added with noticeable resignation.

'And that's exactly what we're going to do,' I announced, energy suddenly coursing through my body. I'd very definitely had enough of lying in the damn grass. 'We'll back off aways, and then swing around to the northeast so that we get ahead of them. That shouldn't be difficult, with the weight they're hauling in that wagon.'

'And *then* what?'

'*Then* you get to play dead.'

I had to hand it to Dan; he made an excellent corpse. His twisted body gave every indication of having suffered a lethal fall from his horse. That creature grazed peacefully nearby, oblivious to the apparent demise of its owner. Hopefully, the sight of such a prize would bring the approaching traders to a halt, but I was painfully aware that my friend had agreed to run a great risk. Such men were unlikely to possess any finer feelings.

I was lying prone on a reverse slope, with my rifle barrel poking through the grass, some thirty yards from the human bait. As the heavily laden vehicle finally came into view, I checked and double-checked the Sharps. I knew that there was likely to be some killing, but genuinely hoped to avoid it. As I had said to Dan, as I reluctantly left him in harm's way, 'Don't forget, we need at least *one* screamer.'

To my fevered mind, it seemed to take an age for the wagon to close in, but even then it abruptly pulled up some fifty yards from Dan's lifeless figure. The three men on the bench seat peered long and hard at the unexpected scene. Then they carefully scrutinised their surroundings and even their back trail, before cautiously advancing. They clutched a variety of weapons, including a sawn-off shotgun, which immediately made me question the wisdom of my scheme. Such a gun could be horrendously destructive at close range, and Dan would have no chance of avoiding its lethal contents. And yet we were well past the point of no return.

At a far slower pace this time, the wagon rattled nearer. Sighting down the Sharps' barrel, I watched intently for any aggressive movement. With my only friend in the world prostrated before the suspicious Indian traders, I could feel beads of sweat forming on my forehead. Then, when the lead oxen were mere feet away from Dan, they drew to a halt. Our intention was that when one of the men climbed down to investigate, the 'dead man' would turn and confront him, whilst I covered the others. What actually happened was that one of the men stood up, pointed his revolver directly at Dan and retracted the hammer to full cock!

As the gunhand made some sidelong comment to his companions and sniggered, I swore vividly and took rapid aim. After squeezing both triggers hard, I had the breechblock lowered before the smoke had even completely cleared. My victim's head exploded like a ripe melon, and his suddenly lifeless body toppled over the side, to land next to one of the large front wheels. Before his cronies had time to react, Dan twisted around to cover them with his cocked revolver. Not anticipating such a move, the man with the shotgun was facing my position, which was definitely the wrong way when armed with such a close quarter weapon. Even though faced with a *fait accompli*, his companion foolishly tried his hand anyway. As the trader attempted to draw a bead on him, Dan fired. The ball struck the man in his right shoulder, causing him to drop his rifle as though it was suddenly red-hot. That left only the individual with the sawn-off.

Rising slightly into view, I called over to him. 'You'll need to get a whole lot closer to me than that, to make that scatter gun pay for its freight!'

The big fellow, who was in fact a magnificent looking character, albeit a half-breed, stared long and hard at me. Then he glanced down at Dan, who had his revolver ready, and finally, with obvious reluctance lowered both hammers and pointed his weapon at the ground. With enormous relief, I clambered to my feet and cautiously approached the wagon. *Our* wagon!

'You! Big man. Climb down off of there,' I commanded. 'Then place the crowd pleaser on the ground and step away from it. Real easy now.'

Only after he had done that did my heartbeat begin to slow. 'You OK, Dan?' I called over.

'Never better,' came the reply. 'But you sure do take some chances with my life!'

I chuckled appreciatively. 'Yeah, well, I'll try not to make it a habit.' Glancing at the body on the far side of the wagon, I asked, 'Is that cuss dead, or just copying you?'

The answer was unequivocal. 'Dead as a wagon tyre. His head's blown six ways from Sunday.'

'The hell with him,' the wounded man suddenly wailed. Blood coated his jacket, and his bearded features registered genuine anguish. 'What about my shoulder? It's hurting something awful. You'd no cause to do this to me. I've never set eyes on either of you in my life.'

Keeping my gun trained on the uninjured trader, I barked out, 'Shuck that gun belt carefully, or I'll put a ball in your other shoulder!'

With only his left arm functioning, it took the wounded man some considerable effort to comply, but eventually it dropped to the ground at his feet.

60

Only now that we were completely in control of the situation did I turn my full attention to the half-breed. 'I see now how you're able to trade with the Sioux,' I remarked, but that individual's expression remained completely deadpan. 'Yet you don't look like the sort of people who could bankroll an outfit like this,' I persisted. 'Which begs the question, who are you working for?'

I might as well have quizzed the man in the moon. His dark eyes didn't even flicker and his mouth remained closed like a trap. 'You'd better start talking,' I snarled. 'Else we'll have to get to beating on you.'

Only then did he finally favour me with a response. The edges of his thin lips curled slightly to form the makings of a sneer. 'You children couldn't make me talk if you had all year.'

Then, very slowly and deliberately, he hoisted his shirt up over his muscular torso. What he revealed rendered me speechless. A vast expanse of livid scar tissue spread around his back and chest. How anyone could have endured such treatment and have survived was beyond me.

'I was captured by the Pawnee,' he explained in a strangely gentle tone. 'They hate the Sioux more than they do you white men, and they knew who had raised me. Those Pawnee worked on me with their knives for a full day, just for the pleasure of it. There was nothing else that they wanted from me, other than to listen to my screams. When they didn't hear any, they grew bored and finally left me alone. That night I managed to escape.' His eyes suddenly settled fully on mine. 'I don't reckon you delicate white boys have got the stomach to dish out that kind of treatment.'

We both knew that he had me, but as ever I was reluctant to back down. Consequently it was some time before I finally shrugged and acknowledged recognition of the fact. Yet his baleful resistance didn't really alter anything, because there was a far easier option available.

'Sit on your hands,' I ordered.

The powerfully built half-breed merely continued to stare at me, without making any movement. He had very obviously concluded that I was a soft touch. With great deliberation, I aimed my Sharps directly at his flat stomach. 'You apparently have a liking for pain,' I remarked almost conversationally. 'So let's see how you handle being gut shot. I'm told it's an awful way to die, and if you ain't going to talk anyway then you're no loss.'

After gazing calculatingly at the gaping muzzle for a few seconds, he slowly lowered himself to the ground, so that a muscular buttock covered each hand. Satisfied, I switched my gaze to the moaning individual on the bench seat. 'Get yourself down here, pronto. You and me are going to have a parley.'

He was a scrawny runt, with smallpox scars just visible above his beard. Tears filled his eyes, and he appeared close to collapse. 'Jesus, Mister. All the strength's gone from my legs,' he wailed.

Turning to Dan, I winked. 'Help him!'

'My pleasure,' he replied, and strode briskly to the wagon. Vaulting up on to a wooden step, he seized the wounded man by his left arm and heaved. Howling with shock, the pathetic individual tumbled to the ground and hit hard. The wind was knocked out of him, and so for a few moments all we heard was rasping breath.

'Why don't you look for that box, Dan?' I hinted. 'I'm sure our new acquaintances ain't gonna give me any trouble.'

As my friend clambered up into the wagon eagerly, I checked the surrounding terrain for unwelcome visitors and then closed in on our injured prisoner. The fall had obviously severely aggravated his shoulder, because his thin features had paled to a chalky whiteness.

'Can you hear me?' I demanded harshly.

Still unable to speak, he nodded shakily. From inside the covered wagon, there came shifting sounds as Dan rummaged through the contents.

'Here's what's gonna happen,' I continued remorselessly. 'You answer my questions, and then we patch you up, and if you're lucky you get to live. How's that sound?'

From off to the side, the half-breed snarled, 'Don't let them get to you, Jase, or you'll answer to me.'

Angrily I swung the Sharps over to cover him. 'Don't press me, *'breed*, or I'll surely drop this hammer on you!' Then, switching my attention back again, I continued with, 'What's it to be, Jase? Greenrod in your shoulder. Stinking, putrid, rotting flesh. That'd be a terrible way for you to shuffle off. Believe me, I've seen it many times in the war.'

Dan's excited voice called out, 'I've found the box, Josiah. It's full of gold Double Eagles! They sure are mighty pretty.'

'Well, well, well,' I crowed, fixing the wounded man with what I hoped was a steely glare. 'Selling guns to the Sioux. The authorities'll surely hang you for that . . . if you live. But if you tell me *everything*, we can maybe do a deal. 'Cause it's not you that we're really after. We want whoever's behind all this. Savvy?'

'All right, all right,' Jase almost screamed. 'What do you want to know?'

The half-breed uttered an almost animal growl, but his suffering crony was too desperate to care.

'Where's all this stuff going?' I demanded.

'To the Missouri, and then on to a steamboat and up to Omaha.'

Now that was a surprise. Omaha was a railroad town, and the Union Pacific's base of operations in the west. 'And then what?' I pressed.

'He gets the strongbox, and we get to keep the hides and tallow. This was the second lot of rifles we had to deliver before the goddamn Sioux would hand it over. They ain't as stupid as white folks like to make out.'

'Who's *he*?'

Jase hesitated nervously for a moment. 'I. . . .'

Before he could say anymore, the half-breed emitted a great roar of anger. 'Silence, you cockchafer!' Twisting sideways, he freed his hands and pulled a knife from his right boot. It wasn't immediately apparent whom his target was, but I wasn't taking any chances. Rapidly swinging my buffalo gun onto his now upright figure, I aimed at his torso and fired.

As the gun crashed out, the big man's body shuddered under the brutal impact of the large calibre ball. We were so close that the embers of the muzzle flash smouldered on his shirt. And yet, despite all that, he somehow remained on his feet. With blood welling up from the wreckage of his chest, he quite unbelievably surged towards me, the knifepoint aimed unerringly at my face.

Instinctively, I swung the butt of my Sharps around so that it smashed solidly into his wrist. There was the distinctive crack of breaking bone, and the blade dropped from his abruptly lifeless fingers. Momentarily off balance, I'm not sure what I would have done next, but thankfully Dan solved my dilemma. A bullet from his Spencer slammed into the huge half-breed's back. After uttering a great moan, he coughed up a torrent of blood and finally collapsed at my feet. As the massive frame twitched its last, I heaved a vast sigh of relief.

'By Christ, he was a beast of a man,' I exclaimed. 'If they're all like him, we'll need a whole regiment to take on that Sioux camp!'

If the sole remaining trader had harboured any

intentions of resisting our demands, they disappeared along with the half-breed's pulse. His next words came in a rush.

'I don't know the son of a bitch's name, but he works for the railroad.'

Dan and I exchanged startled glances, but we were given no chance to comment.

'He's a dapper little prick, though. No sweaty, dirty work for him. Real carriage trade. I've never afore seen such a dude!'

That description had my pulse racing again. 'When I met with Dodge,' I remarked to my friend, 'There was just such a dude in the railroad car.' Then to Jase, 'Does he tote a thin little moustache?'

This time the trader nodded slowly, and with a great show of reluctance. Although obviously in immense pain, he appeared suddenly wary about where this was leading, and what my knowing this individual might signify. I reloaded my long gun pensively, conscious of having stupidly said too much.

'What does all this mean?' Dan asked nervously.

'Later!' I responded shortly. 'First off, you need to help me with this bull turd.' So saying, I returned my full attention to the trader.

Abject fear leapt into his eyes. 'What are you about?' he bleated.

'We made a deal, remember?' I replied. 'We're going to patch up that shoulder of yourn. Can't have you bleeding over the deck of a steamboat, can we?'

'Say what?' he queried incredulously.

I smiled reassuringly. 'You've got two new partners. Let's hope for your sake that you don't go the way of the others!'

CHAPTER SIX

'What happened to him?'

'He met with an accident.'

'Uhuh.' The steamboat captain was unimpressed. He'd obviously seen it all during his time on the river. Nevertheless, his eyes lingered on Jase's slight figure, as that man lounged disconsolately on the lower deck of the sternwheeler *Bertrand*. 'This ain't the first time he's made this trip, you know. And the fellas that done travelled with him last time didn't seem like the sort you'd take issue with. A bit like you, only meaner looking . . . and one of them was a breed. You never can trust them sons of bitches!'

I scrutinized the captain long and hard, and finally decided that I might as well take a chance on him. The two of us stood on the upper deck, home to the luxurious staterooms that generated the real profit for the boat's owners. Since Dan and I had unexpectedly come into funds, I had treated the two of us to a journey in style. I didn't consider it thievery, so much as a claim for expenses. 'They met with accidents as well,' I eventually replied.

The captain's eyes twinkled as he chuckled wryly. 'Theirs must have been a real dangerous line of work.'

'I'll cut to the chase, Captain. . . ?'

'Yore. James Yore.'

'My name's Joe Wakefield, Captain Yore. Me and Dan work for the Union Pacific Railroad. You may have heard of it,' I added teasingly. 'That fella below is our prisoner. Him and the others were up to something real unpleasant . . . until their bad deeds caught up with them. It might help us if you could recall anything about them. What they did. Who they saw.'

Yore viewed me with interest. 'Seems to me anyone could say they work for the Union Pacific, but you seem like a decent young fella, so I'll take you on good faith an' tell you one thing for sure. They didn't have no heavy strongbox with them. And I ain't the only cuss on this boat that's noticed it. If I was you, I'd be mighty careful with it when you disembark. Else somebody might just try to take it away from you. Which would be kind of a shame, 'cause there's already too much skulduggery on this river.'

'What's mine ain't easy to take,' I retorted. 'But I'm obliged for the warning.'

'As for those other fellas, well, I didn't take a right lot of notice of them,' Yore continued. 'Although I did buy some tallow off them. It makes good grease for the engines. I'll do the same deal with you, if you wish.'

Engine grease was the last thing on my mind. 'When they reached Omaha, did you happen to notice anything unusual?'

The other man grunted. 'There's little that's usual on the Missouri, but yeah, one thing struck me. They were met by some snooty looking bastard in a carriage. Seemed to me like he wouldn't even piss on the likes of them if they were on fire, and yet they all had plenty to jaw about.'

Before I could comment, the boat's steam horn blasted out above us, and then the captain was approached by one of the crew. There were matters that needed his attention up in the wheelhouse, and so I was left alone to ponder his words. Glancing past the idlers at the rail, I surveyed the immense brown sweep of river as the *Bertrand* fought her way up it against the strong current. Proof of the effort required came in the form of great plumes of black smoke billowing from the two high chimneys near the front of the boat. At the rear, the single massive paddlewheel churned relentlessly through the water. Modern steam technology was indeed a wondrous thing.

We would soon be arriving at Omaha's landing stage, and so I decided to probe our prisoner a little more. If it was indeed Dodge's mysterious companion who awaited the traders' arrival, then there could well be some awkward moments ahead, and I had yet to decide on a course of action.

Turning away, I made my way down the steps to the far less salubrious surroundings of the lower deck. Our 'merchandise' was still loaded in the wagon. That, along with its team and our horses was all on deck, in company with a great deal of other cargo, which didn't allow a whole lot of space for the human passengers. With the *Bertrand* being shallow drafted, there just wasn't the hold space that one would expect to find in a seagoing vessel. And now, with water lapping over the gunwales, the craft seemed dangerously overloaded. But then what did I know? I was just a landlubber, but still glad that the strongbox was on the upper deck, in our statcroom next to Dan's bed. He was resting in there with the cocked Spencer in his lap.

The scrawny Indian trader glanced at me sourly when I fetched up next to him. His shoulder wound had not yet shown any signs of infection, but we had been unable to extract the misshapen ball, and he was obviously in a great deal of discomfort. It would be up to a sawbones to see to him, and since we needed the trader's testimony, we would doubtless have to pay for the treatment.

'What the hell kind of name is Jase, anyhu?' I asked this more as an opener than out of any real fascination.

He hawked up some yellow phlegm onto the deck. 'My given name is Jason, but never mind that shit because for sure you ain't interested. I've been doing me some thinking while I've been sitting here rotting. Look at all these people. How are you gonna stop me just walking off this damn boat in Omaha? You can't just gun down a wounded, unarmed man like a dog!'

I shrugged. 'Maybe, maybe not. But if I told all

these good folks how you've been selling guns and whiskey to the Sioux, d'you reckon anyone'll try to stop me? Or will they be queuing up to put a bullet in your worthless hide?'

For the first time that day his brow furrowed with anger rather than pain. 'You miserable goddamned cockroach. . . .'

The jarring crash was so sudden and so extreme that it literally threw me off my feet. All around me fellow passengers were tossed to the deck like rag dolls. Others who weren't so lucky struck the rail and were pitched over it into the Missouri. Animals struggled to free themselves, and Jase howled with agony as he tumbled down on his injured shoulder.

For an awful moment I thought that there had been a boiler explosion. Such an occurrence was common on riverboats; they usually resulted in horrendous burns and scalds for those lucky enough to survive. Then I realized that to have stopped so suddenly, the *Bertrand* had to have struck a hidden obstruction, maybe one of the many dead trees that I had seen in the river. As I got shakily to my feet, I peered over the side. Sweet Jesus, the boat was not only stopped, it was sinking, and with the weight on board it wouldn't take long!

From the wheelhouse, Captain Yore bellowed out, 'She's going down. Swim for your lives!'

'That's easy for him to say,' Jase protested. His pain-filled eyes were like saucers as he took in the pandemonium around him. Since passengers on the lower deck were mostly poor, they had few possessions to worry about and so were quick to make for the side rails. It was likely to be a different story on the level above, especially as much of the deck cargo belonged to the stateroom passengers as well.

'I'll help you,' I replied. 'But first I've got to find Dan.' Without waiting for a response, I was off at a run.

After fighting through the throng, I bounded up the steps to the upper deck. Anxiously approaching our stateroom door, I still had the presence of mind to knock on it first and call out. I had no intention of bursting in without warning and taking a bullet. As the door opened, I was greatly relieved to find my friend standing before me. He had an ugly bruise on his forehead, but otherwise appeared to be unhurt.

'I only went and fell against the goddamned strong-box,' he complained.

'The boat's sinking,' I announced. 'The animals'll have to fend for themselves. And there's nothing we can do about the hides and tallow, but we have to save the Double Eagles.'

'How?' Dan retorted. 'We can't swim with the box, and that's for sure.'

I'd already arrived at that conclusion, but I had also already thought of the saddles and gear in our stateroom.

'We'll use the lariats on the saddles to fasten a line to the box and then carry it outside. All we have to do is swim ashore, and then drag it off the boat and over

73

to the bank.'

'Don't you ever worry you might run out of ideas?' Dan snapped, but nevertheless he was smiling broadly.

With the boat visibly settling in the water, there was apparently not a moment to lose. By tying both lengths of rope together, we soon had a line long enough to easily reach the Missouri's west bank, which was the side that Omaha was situated on. Although the Sioux had smashed the strongbox's lock, lengths of rawhide that were easily up to the job had replaced it.

With our long guns slung over our shoulders, we each seized a handle and carried the heavy box down to the lower deck. With water beginning to lap on to it, and many passengers already in the river and desperately swimming for safety, nobody paid us any mind . . . except for Jase.

'What about me?' he whined. The little runt was already shivering, as though in anticipation of a cold dip. 'I can't swim with this shoulder. You shot me, now you'll have to save me.'

'Aw, stop bellyaching,' I replied. 'Happen you need a bath, and I'll stay with you. You'll be fine. Dan, get going. We'll follow on.'

Nodding briskly, my companion tied one end of the line around his waist and slipped over the side. As we looked on, he struck out strongly for the bank, the rope uncoiling behind him. Nevertheless, in the grip of the current and burdened by his weapons, he soon found himself being carried downriver along with

many others. Not all were good swimmers, and desperate pleas for help sounded off around the boat.
Panic-stricken animals joining the throng com-
pounded the mayhem.

A few individuals, seeing the danger, decided to
gamble on the depth of the river and risk staying on
the boat. They headed for the upper deck and ulti-
mately the wheelhouse. Rightly or wrongly I had made
my choice, and that meant following Dan. He was now
benefiting from being tethered to the heavy box,
because it had acted as an anchor against the current,
and was aiding his dash for the shore. I suddenly
became aware that my boots were wet, and water was
lapping at the strongbox. It was time to go.

'Jump in,' I barked at the terrified Indian trader, as
I slung the Sharps across my back.

'I changed my mind,' he mumbled. 'Those fellas up
there might have the right of it, and I ain't no fish.'

'You are now,' I opined, and gave him a solid shove.

With a cry of alarm, Jase fell forward into the river.
After a final glance at the strongbox I followed him in,
and Christ but it was cold. Completely immersed, the
chill momentarily took my breath away. Then my head
and shoulders broke the surface and I kicked out vigorously. Yet something was badly amiss.

'Jase, where are you?' I yelled. Frantically twisting
around in search of him, I just managed to avoid a
fast-moving tree branch, before realizing with a
sinking heart that the little shit was nowhere to be
seen. Cursing, I ducked under the water, straining to

catch sight of him. Unbelievably, there was just no sign. He had completely disappeared. I could only think that he had got into trouble under water and been carried off by the current.

'Damn, damn, damn,' I intoned. His worthless life meant nothing in the overall scheme of things, but he would have made a useful witness once we caught up with the ringleader. Now all we had was a box of Double Eagles . . . *if* we could get it ashore. After a last search, I followed in the thrashing wake of so many other shocked survivors. My sodden clothes and heavy weapons dragged at me, but finally I reached the west bank. Clawing at tufts of grass, I hauled my weary body out of the Missouri. That was one boat trip I wouldn't forget in a hurry!

As I drew in deep draughts of air thankfully, I searched for my friend. Surely he hadn't succumbed as well? Then I spotted him, further up the bank towards Omaha. My hunt for Jase, coupled with the lack of a tether, meant that I had drifted further down-river with the current. My relief turned to admiration as I watched Dan vigorously hauling on the rope, which was mostly concealed under the surface. Knowing that I really should help him, I wearily got to my feet and plodded heavily towards him.

'What happened to that little bastard?' he queried as I finally joined him.

'He didn't make it,' I remarked with self-serving regret. 'The ball you put in him must have weighed too much.'

'Hmm, a bit like these goddamn coins,' he retorted breathlessly. 'How about a little help here?'

Together we heaved on the rope, and bit-by-bit the strongbox edged towards us on the river bottom. Sometimes it snagged on a rock, only to break free when we employed more effort. Further down the bank, men struggled ashore, gasping and exhausted, but we completely ignored them. We had far more important considerations. For what seemed an age, we kept on pulling, until quite suddenly the box appeared in the shallows. Amazingly it appeared to be undamaged.

'Thank Christ for that,' I exclaimed. Surely after all this, nothing else could go wrong.

'We'll be taking that now!' The voice had a dangerous edge to it that hinted at deadly force backing it up. And so it proved.

Warily, we both turned to view the speaker. He was a big fellow with the appearance of a barroom brawler, only in this case one who had taken a prolonged bath. His far smaller partner possessed a similar demeanour, and both men were covering us with cocked revolvers.

'Looking at all the effort you both put in,' the bruiser continued, 'There must be an awful lot of something in that box. So what you're gonna do is shuck all that iron you're packing and just walk away.' A faint smile played on his hard features, as though he was supremely confident that he held the upper hand. 'That's right. We ain't even gonna kill you . . . unless you're fool enough to turn ornery!'

Dan and I glanced meaningfully at each other. There was no chance of any outside help. The soaking survivors of yet another river disaster had their own problems to think on. It was beginning to seem as if we had transgressed in a former life, and that it was now pay back time. Then something occurred to me that brought a smile to my face. Perusing the opportunist's gun hand, I saw water dripping from it and came to a rapid conclusion.

'Seems to me you're overlooking something,' I remarked coolly. 'That Colt Army's just had a prolonged ducking, and black powder really doesn't take well to water. Even if the cap's still sound, I reckon the chambers'll be full of black paste by now.'

I stared at him long and hard, until suddenly his left eye twitched ever so slightly, and I knew then that I had him. Without warning, I shrugged the captured Henry from my shoulder and levered up a round. 'On the other hand, this long gun's crammed full of copper cartridges that I loaded last *Sunday*.' Since he completely missed my war veteran's attempt at wry humour, I quickly continued with, 'In time they might turn green, but right now I'd bet everything in this box that it'll blow a hole in your addled skull.'

His stoop shouldered crony, who so far hadn't said a word, licked his lips nervously and exchanged a sidelong glance with his buddy. 'You reckon he's joshing with us?'

'Shut your mouth!' the plug-ugly snarled.

'So, what's it to be?' I rasped.

'Happen we might could have made a mistake,' the leader finally allowed. Then, very carefully, he eased the hammer down. Mumbling something unintelligible, the other fellow followed suit.

I nodded with satisfaction, but I wasn't finished with them quite yet. 'Anything that you've got that spits lead, in the river with it!'

'Whaaat?' exclaimed the would-be river pirate incredulously. 'You can't leave us defenceless. We might fall in with bad company.'

'You already have,' I remarked, and then lowering the Henry's barrel, I squeezed the trigger. With a thoroughly satisfying crash, the rifle discharged. The bullet tore through the faded leather of his right boot and on into the ground, leaving bloody wreckage in its path.

'You bastard,' my victim howled. 'You've shot my toe off!' Such was his incandescent rage that he actually appeared ready to again chance his hand with the cap 'n' ball Colt.

Rapidly working the lever action, I switched my aim to his other foot. 'This really is a peach of a gun. So unless you want a matching pair, heave your iron into the river. Well out, so that it stays lost.'

With tears in his eyes, the luckless fellow finally saw sense and tossed his revolver into the Missouri. Following his lead, his partner did the same and provoked a cry of outrage from an evacuee still struggling in the water. The heavy firearm had missed the swimmer by a hair's breadth.

'Now you two cockchafers get out of my sight,' I commanded. 'If I see you again, I'll kill you!'

Plainly seething with anger and resentment, the two men turned away and headed off upriver towards Omaha, watched by a crowd of bemused survivors. The big one hobbled badly and had to keep stopping to seek some relief.

'Hot dang. You sure showed them,' Dan crowed exultantly.

'Yeah. Yeah, I did, didn't I?' I responded rather more pensively. 'I just hope they don't turn up as tracklayers at the railhead, or I might just have to come good on that threat.'

Dan blinked with surprise at the prospect. 'Yeah, well. They shouldn't try robbing folks.' He paused. 'So, what happens now?'

'*Now*, one of us walks to Omaha to rent a buggy, giving those two pus weasels a wide berth, of course. Although I reckon the one I hobbled will be sat with his foot in the river for a fair while. Whoever stays here guards this box against any more road agents *and* gets to have a rest.' I favoured him with a sly smile that really should have given him pause. 'We just have to decide as to who does what, is all.'

'Let's toss a coin,' Dan suggested brightly. 'Hell, we've got plenty of them. And besides, I'm feeling lucky!'

As my companion trudged north unhappily, I sat on

the strongbox and pocketed the double-headed dollar coin that I had purchased as a useful novelty whilst in the Union army. It hadn't really been fair of me to take advantage of my friend, but I couldn't resist a chuckle. He was younger than me and the exercise would do him good!

All around me, the mostly male passengers were coming to a certain conclusion, and that was that they should maybe have stayed on the *Bertrand*. The steamboat had apparently settled on the bottom, with the wheelhouse and most of the upper deck still visible. The more affluent evacuees had left a great many possessions in the staterooms that those still on board could easily plunder.

Then I caught sight of Captain Yore, observing me from the wheelhouse. Strangely, he was brandishing a sawn-off shotgun, which appeared to be for the sole benefit of the few remaining passengers. I could only presume that the deadly weapon was to enforce the rule of law on board. Nevertheless, I couldn't resist bellowing over to him. 'Why did you order us to swim for it, when you must have known the depth of the water?'

The captain took only a moment to consider. 'Well, I'll tell you, young fella,' he hollered back. 'This is one river man that don't aim to die poor. I've got to say though, you did right well getting that box off of here and then keeping hold of it. It bespeaks of a great deal of wealth, and I reckon I'll be the loser because of that.' And with that he roared with laughter.

'Well, it looks like you get our tallow for free, anyhu,' I retorted. 'That's if you manage to salvage it.'

That made him laugh all the louder, but since we had managed to keep hold of the gold, I decided that whatever scheme he had cooked up, good luck to him. If nothing else, he seemed like an amiable rogue. Then a far darker thought occurred to me. What if he had deliberately wrecked the *Bertrand* purely for personal gain? Now that really would be something to think on!

CHAPTER SEVEN

Darkness was falling by the time we reached Omaha, a fact that suited my purpose entirely. Whilst waiting for Dan to return, I had given our situation a deal of thought. Unfortunately, the negative aspects of it far outweighed the positive. We had survived our first mission for the Union Pacific's Chief Engineer, and had a box of Double Eagles to show for it, but sadly I no longer knew whom I could trust. And that included General Dodge!

Pitch torches flared in the street, and oil lamps flickered in the massive Cozzens House Hotel as we rode the buggy over to the livery stables that it had been hired from. The illumination favoured the frontier city with a warm glow that was entirely missing from my soul. I was beginning to formulate a plan of sorts, but felt myself to be inundated with potential enemies on all sides.

Luckily for us, the arrival of the Union Pacific had changed Omaha irrevocably. It was now a bustling city of well over twenty thousand souls, and growing all the time. Seven steamboats were permanently employed on the Missouri River, bringing in rolling stock, supplies and ever more workers. All of this meant that anyone searching for us would have their work cut out. It was also a fact that for some people, simple needs always took priority.

'I sure could use a drink of Old Red Eye,' Dan announced with feeling. 'It cuts through the dust better than all that damn river water I swallowed.'

'Well, you might just have to wait a little bit longer for that,' I responded regretfully. 'We need to keep our heads down until I figure out what to do.' Seeing his disappointment, I added, 'It sure is a shame we didn't get to remain in that stateroom, because I guess we'll be sleeping in the livery tonight, but we'll send a stable hand out to fetch a jug. How's that sound?'

His great beaming smile was acknowledgement enough, and despite the situation I had no option but to return it. Although he left all the decisions to me, I couldn't have wanted for a better companion than Dan Sturgis. More than ever, I felt glad to have retained his friendship after our disagreement back at the railhead.

It was later that evening when Dan's whiskey finally arrived from a saloon on 9th Street, but that wasn't the only thing that the old stable hand brought with him. He also had some very unsettling news.

'You're not the only fellas in town to have come off

the *Bertrand.* There's a lot of angry passengers getting liquored up and jawing on about lynching its captain. If they ever get to find him, that is. Seems he was in league with a gang of river pirates who fetched up in a boat to clean out the staterooms. Hee, hee. That tickled me when I heard it. There's some folks you've just got to admire.'

The grizzled old coot leered at us for a moment, as though pondering something. We were all ensconced in the semi-darkness of an empty stall, and he seemed in no hurry to resume his chores. 'There's also a story going around about two young men toting a box full of gold bars . . . or was it coins? Darned if I can remember. But anyhu, if all of that ain't enough, there's some real hard cases in town who seem to believe it. As though they was *expecting* them. The gold, that is.' With that, he scratched his hairy chin and awaited our response.

As my heart sank, I shook my head in dismay. Things just seemed to be going from bad to worse. 'What's your name, old-timer?'

'Percy.'

'Well, Percy,' I began. 'I guess I've got to ask whether you said anything to those *hard cases,* and if you haven't yet, are you likely to be tempted to? No offence intended.'

'None taken,' he responded, before chuckling softly. 'An' you needn't go sweating on my account. I'm too old to care about blood money, and talk of gold and shit like that. *And* I ain't partial to bully boys throwing their weight around either. Besides, you

85

seem like a couple of nice young fellas, even if you are dragging some kind of strongbox around with you. So I guess that all means they couldn't buy me for money, marbles or chalk, but I right fancy a sip of that joy juice I've just fetched in for you.'

Sighing with relief, it was my turn to chuckle. 'Go right ahead and help yourself, Percy. In fact, take the whole jug and enjoy. We're going to need clear heads tomorrow, so we've had our fill. Haven't we, Dan?'

My friend coloured slightly, before shrugging. 'If you say so . . . I guess. Personally I was just getting a taste for it.'

The stable hand got to his feet, jug in hand. 'I'll leave you boys to make your plans. What I don't know can't hurt me, huh?' With that, he wandered off contently to the front of the livery. It was very obvious that he was left to his own devices for long periods of time, which suited me entirely.

I shifted my gaze to Dan. 'Seems to me that the safest place for us is at the railhead. I really don't see Jack Casement being involved in all this, and I sure could use his advice.'

'Fair enough,' Dan agreed. 'But just how are we gonna get there, lugging this box about, an' all?'

I laughed, because that was the easy part. 'By train, of course. We work for the Union Pacific, don't we? We'll spend the night in here, and then hitch a lift on the morning supply run.'

Dan shook his head in mock wonder. 'You always make it sound so easy, Josiah!'

*

I was jerked awake from a sound shuteye by the sound of raised voices. Even though fogged with sleep, I was still able to recognize one of them.

'You got no call waking me up like this,' Percy protested, his words noticeably slurred.

'You give us any trouble, old man, an' you won't ever wake up again,' came the uncompromising response.

Instinctively I just knew that this intrusion had to be connected with us. As a deep chill settled on me, I crawled over to Dan and placed a hand firmly over his mouth. His eyes snapped open and he began to struggle, until he made out my features in the dim light.

'Get to the back of the stall and under the hay,' I whispered. 'No shooting unless I say so.'

As my friend complied, the unknown voice continued with, 'You had any strangers in here today?'

Percy's head was obviously clearing, because he offered a quick retort. 'This is a stables. We get folks coming and going every day.' There was a momentary silence, followed by a sharp cry of pain.

'Don't get cute with me, gramps. I got questions that need answers, an' if I don't get the right ones, it'll go badly for you.'

Easing my head around the end of the stall, I peered over to the large open area near the front of the stables. Percy had been lying on a pile of hay near the entrance, sleeping off the free rotgut. Now he was on his feet, surrounded by three menacing figures. The leader of these thugs obviously knew his business, and that boded ill for the old stable hand . . . unless he disclosed our presence swiftly. And there really was no good reason why he shouldn't do that.

'You might not know this,' continued his interrogator remorselessly, 'but earlier today a steamboat ran aground just south of here. There's talk of two survivors heading this way in a buggy, toting a real heavy box. And the only place in this burg that rents buggies is the livery. This livery! So I'm gonna ask you again: have you had any strangers in here today?' The moment that he finished speaking, he nodded at one of his cronies. That man reacted by kicking Percy's feet from under him, and the helpless liveryman collapsed to the floor. It took him a moment or two to recover his wind.

'OK, OK, enough,' he finally cried out loudly. 'I'll spill the beans.'

I possessed enough wit to realize that he was announcing his intentions. He was giving us the chance to at least attempt an escape. Then something happened that altered everything. Suddenly confident that they were on to something, the three plug-uglies shifted position around his prone body, so that they could also keep an eye on the rest of the building. As they did so, I got a clear view of one of their faces in the lamplight. Although badly in need of a shave, there was no disguising the fact that it was lean and sallow.

'Elijah!' I exclaimed only barely under my breath. So my former employee was now working as a hired thug. The question was, who for? Twisting around, I scrambled to the rear of the stall. 'The time for hiding's gone,' I whispered rapidly, unsheathing my knife. 'One of those pus weasels is our very own Elijah, his back turned on honest work. I'll not run from the likes of him. When Percy gets to jawing again, we're gonna take them at a rush. Without any gunplay mind, but remember, they're here to do us harm, so fight mean. Are you with me?'

Dan clambered to his feet, and drew his skinning knife. 'That's a hell of a thing to ask me, Josiah Wakefield!'

Over at the front of the building, the ringleader prompted the stable hand with a sharp kick. 'Well, out with it.'

The time for dissembling had gone. 'Some young fella turned up this afternoon. His clothes were still damp and he asked to hire a buggy. He had coin to pay, so he got what he wanted. Later on, two of them returned . . . with a heavy box, but I never saw what was in it. Honest, Mister.'

As we left the stall silently, conveniently all eyes were exclusively on Percy. 'And then what?' came the entirely predictable question.

To give him his due, the old soak gave us every chance to make our move. Drawing out each word, he replied, 'You . . . won't . . . believe . . . this, but . . . they're . . . still. . . .'

And then we were on them. Slamming into the back of the leader, I seized his lank hair, heaved his head back, and sliced my blade deep into his neck. Drowning abruptly in his own blood, the helpless thug didn't even get chance to cry out. Dan's prey was already on the turn when he reached him, so he had to content himself with jabbing his blade up to the hilt in a soft belly. As that man howled in agony, my friend forced him to the ground so as to smother his cries. And then I lost sight of him, because I was desperately conscious that we had taken on more than two gun thugs. Using my victim as a barrier, I turned to confront Elijah, my right hand now greasy with blood.

The blow that struck my face full on had some real heft behind it. With pain exploding in my head, I toppled back, taking the dead man with me. Landing on the hard floor with him on top forced all the air out of my lungs, leaving me as powerless as a baby. Elijah drew his Colt Army to finish the job, but was momentarily stymied by my human shield. Then he caught sight of my bloodied features in the lamplight and froze with surprise.

'Sweet Jesus, Wakefield!'

That short reprieve doubtless saved my life, because before he could act further, Dan delivered a doozy of a sockdologer to the back of his head. Elijah grunted and crumpled to the floor, joining everyone other than my companion.

Percy, unhurt and emboldened by the one-sided violence, was the first to get back on his feet. 'Hot dang! You two sure lit into those fellas,' he acknowledged appreciatively.

I had floods of tears in my eyes, and blood and snot trickling over my jaw. I was convinced that my nose was broken, which didn't sit well with me at all.

As Dan heaved me upright, he seemed to be of the same opinion. 'That Elijah's busted you up pretty good!'

Tentatively, I gently felt my battered features. In truth, nothing appeared to be moving that shouldn't be, and I abruptly decided to leave well alone. There were, after all, far more important matters to consider. We now had two dead men on our hands, and the fate of a third to chew over. That fact was already working on Dan.

'Jesus, I can't believe it's come to this,' he opined. 'What the hell are we gonna do with Elijah? We can't just murder him in cold blood, can we? *Can we?*'

Killing with a blade is about as intimate as it gets, so I understood his indecision entirely. When you live and work with a man, even for just a few weeks, everything becomes personal. So no, we couldn't just slice Elijah up like a piece of meat. The other two had been different. They were merely nameless thugs.

'We sure as hell can't leave him here, though,' I finally responded. Christ, my nose felt like it had taken an anvil strike. 'Once he talks, he'll bring someone's wrath down on Percy, and we can't allow that. So if we can't kill him and we can't dump him, that means he's coming to the railhead with us. Who knows, he might stop a bullet meant for us. Now that would be justice!'

So it was decided. We would remain in the stables until just before first light, and then, borrowing the buggy again, would transport our prisoner and the gold over to the railroad yard. Once on the supply train we would travel to the railhead and . . . do what exactly? That was my problem. Who could I trust?

'What about these two stiffs?' Dan queried. 'Ain't they gonna cause you all kinds of trouble, Percy?'

'Nah,' the old-timer remarked dismissively. 'This town's become a cesspit. Murders are commonplace. Time was I knew everyone living here by sight, but that's all changed now. The railroad's to blame. So anyone asks, I'll just say I slept through the night after supping all this joy juice.'

I patted him on the shoulder gratefully. 'You're a good man, Percy,' I remarked with genuine warmth. Then to Dan I added, 'Let's get this cockchafer securely tied up before he comes to. And a kerchief around his mouth wouldn't go amiss, either. We don't want him bringing any more trouble down around us.'

'Then what do we do 'til daybreak?' Dan asked.

To me, the answer was blindingly obvious. Indicating the two cadavers, I replied, 'Those sons of bitches interrupted my shuteye. Both of us could use some more. So if I was you I'd hit the hay, unless all this blood bothers you.'

'Only my own,' was his glib response. 'Although I'll allow that your face could benefit from some work.'

I spat a mixture of blood and phlegm on to the floor ruefully before going in search of a water bucket. 'And ain't that the truth!'

CHAPTER EIGHT

The short journey through the quiet streets to the extensive railroad yard had proved uneventful. As expected, the heavily laden supply train was almost ready to depart. The fireman had been feeding the boiler whilst the engineer checked the pressure. My mention of Jack Casement's name, plus our own determined demeanour, silenced any objections to our presence from the crew. The fact that one of our number was bound and gagged only seemed to emphasize our bona fides. As a result, the three of us were now ensconced on a vast flatbed railroad car, surrounded by wooden crossties and iron rails. We were midway along the train, and so identical loads stretched off in either direction. There were no passenger carriages connected to it, which meant that other than the engine crew, we were the only people on board. Dan had tied Elijah to a thirty-foot iron rail weighing roughly six hundred pounds, so there was no possibility of his escaping.

As the long supply train built up speed, black sooty smoke from the vertical smokestack was swept back on the wind, and I recalled just how unpleasant railroad travel could be. Wood burners were even worse, because flying sparks would often land on unlucky travellers. And yet, despite all that, it sure beat the hell out of riding to the distant railhead.

It wasn't until our mechanised transport had left Omaha's city limits well behind that we got around to unfastening Elijah's gag. And this time there was no evidence of his taciturn nature.

'You dirty, lousy, stinking bastards! You got no call to beat on me and tie me up this way.'

I regarded him with a total lack of sympathy, prompted by continued discomfort. 'We're supposed to let you plug us with lead then, is that it? And besides, look what you've done to my damn face!'

Elijah contemptuously spat on the floor. 'That's nothing. My boss says you've got an awful lot of something that don't belong to you. Because of your dodgy dealings, he's out of pocket, big style.'

'Hah,' I retorted. 'And just who is your boss?'

Elijah's eyes narrowed. 'Wouldn't you just like to know?'

I sighed. I actually wanted to know very badly, but I had a headache and really wasn't in the mood for games. 'Fasten that gag back on him, Dan. Nice and tight,' I ordered. 'We're wasting our time.'

Our prisoner definitely wasn't keen on that idea. 'OK, OK. Just let's jaw a bit more. I won't sass you any.'

I regarded him balefully. 'As I recall, you weren't usually one for conversation.'

He scowled, took a deep breath and tried again. 'Is that really gold you've got in that box?'

Recognizing the mixture of greed and curiosity on his face, I decided that perhaps it was time to try a different tack. 'Yes. Yes it is. But it belongs to the Union Pacific Railroad. It was taken by the Sioux in a raid, and whoever you're working for knew this. He supplied them with repeating rifles in exchange for the gold and other things, knowing that he'd make a massive profit. The fact that men are dying because of it doesn't seem to matter to him.'

Elijah gazed at me in bewilderment. 'But what's all this got to do with you two? You're just buffalo hunters . . . ain't you?'

'Not anymore,' Dan answered, his chest swelling slightly with pride. 'Ever since that Sioux raid on the railhead, me and Josiah have been working for General Dodge. We're Indian fighters now!'

As my former employee absorbed all this, I determined that it was time to pile on the pressure. 'You've fallen in with a bad lot, Elijah, and you could yet swing for it. Our problem is that we don't know just whom we're up against. That's why we fled Omaha. I reckon we'll be a mite safer at the railhead. If you renounce your bad ways and help us, I'll speak up for you. But first I need to know who your boss is.'

'Too thin, Joe. Too thin,' he proclaimed. 'If I tell you what I know, that puts me in danger as well. He'll think I've sided with you. I need guarantees. Something in writing from the top man. And you can start off by untying me.'

With Dan waiting expectantly at my side, I stared long and hard at our devious prisoner. I had always suspected that he was far from a fool. What he knew would definitely assist us, but could I trust him not to stab me in the back at the first opportunity? 'Gag him,' I commanded.

'You low-down, rotten. . .' The material rammed back in his mouth choked off any more vitriol.

Disappointed that I had not made any real headway with Elijah, I glanced around at the surrounding terrain. It was gratifyingly empty of any potential enemies. The engine had a full head of steam and we were making good time. We would reach the railhead well before noon. What kind of reception we would get was another matter entirely.

'I've just realized something,' Dan piped up brightly. 'We've damn nearly completed a full circuit. South to the Sioux camp. East to the Missouri River. Then north to Omaha, and now we're heading west, back to the railhead! Don't that just beat all!'

Despite our circumstances and the pain in my head, I had to laugh out loud. 'Yes, Dan, I guess it does!'

In spite of the constant clatter, both on and under the railroad cars, we had both drifted off to sleep under the warm sun, safe in the knowledge that our captive wasn't going anywhere. Therefore the strident and maddeningly repetitive steam whistle came as a nerve shredding shock. Added to the din was the screeching of brakes, as our supply train slowed down noticeably. I could only imagine that we had slept for the rest of the journey, and that the railhead was now before us. What I actually saw came as one hell of a jolt.

There wasn't another human in sight. Instead, spread out before us, was a huge herd of buffalo, numbering into the thousands. The great, shaggy beasts had engulfed the railroad track, and showed little concern for the impatient, snorting Iron Horse that they had effectively halted.

As the train finally came to a grinding halt, I clambered to my feet. This was ridiculous. Mankind's most definitive invention brought to a standstill by a horde of primitive beasts. Glancing over at the engine, I caught sight of the fireman in the cab and bellowed over. 'What's to be done?'

'There's too many to just plough through them,' he hollered back. 'All we can do is blow the whistle and edge forward. This happens to us all the time.'

The way he said that last bit implied that they just had to accept the situation, but that wasn't near good enough for me. I knew a thing or two about buffalo, and wasn't inclined to wait on their whims. Gesturing with my Sharps, I replied, 'I haven't got time for this. I'll drop a couple of them near the track. That should spook the rest and get them on the move.'

The startled fireman threw a salute at me, and turned away to inform the engineer. Cocking my weapon, I took aim at one of the creatures grazing peacefully near the locomotive. This was too easy. In the past, I had needed to keep my distance, so as not to alarm them, whereas now that was precisely the intention. With the butt tucked tightly into my shoulder, I drew in a breath, held it, and. . . .

An abrupt cacophony of noise emanated from our left flank, and quite suddenly a herd of buffalo was the least of our worries. A large party of mounted Indians had come out of nowhere, and there could be no doubt as to their hostile intentions. In fact, it was quite probable that they had spotted the position of the herd on the railroad track and had decided to lie in wait. Uttering savage cries, they pounded towards what they thought would be easy pickings.

Cursing, I squeezed both triggers, and was rewarded by a buffalo collapsing on the spot. The other animals stirred uneasily and began to edge away from the hissing steam engine. Rapidly, I recharged the breechloader, before roughly yanking the gag out of Elijah's mouth.

'We're going to be fighting for our lives in a minute. If we cut you free, are you with us or against us?'

It took mere seconds for the other man to make up his mind, because he too had heard the lurid stories of Indian atrocities. 'With you, goddamn it,' he barked out. 'But I'll need a gun!'

'Cut him free,' I snapped at Dan. 'Give him your Spencer, and take this Henry.' Since I still didn't really trust Elijah, it made sense to at least give him the slower of the two repeaters.

As the freed prisoner painfully stretched his aching limbs, I dropped another of the big shaggies, and abruptly the whole herd was on the move. 'Get us the hell out of here,' I hollered at the engine.

Even over the noise in the cab, the crew had spotted the war party, and needed no further urging. The fireman grabbed his shovel and began frantically feeding the firebox, whilst the engineer set about working the control levers. As I reloaded again, the train began to move, but there was a tremendous amount of weight to pull. Instinctively, I realized that the Sioux would be upon us before we got up to speed. The buffalo were fleeing in a different direction, and so sadly would not hinder the approaching warriors.

My companions had not yet opened fire. Sensibly they had waited for the fast moving horsemen to get within easy range. 'Fire at the animals,' I commanded. 'All we need to do is hold them off until we're moving again.'

A ragged volley erupted from behind the iron rails, taking the warriors completely by surprise. Three ponies went down in agony, taking their riders with them. Startled at the unexpected resistance, the rest of them veered off and began to aim their own repeating rifles. Their horsemanship was simply superb, leading Elijah to offer a sour and very probably envious comment.

'Who the hell do they think they are? The lords of

the plains?'

Bullets flew in our direction, but a pile of iron rails made for an excellent fortress, and none of us were injured. As the train began to pick up speed, the Sioux continued with their original plan. Ignoring us, they raced on to the locomotive, and began to fire into the cab. Recognizing that if they killed the crew, we were all in big trouble, I came to a rapid decision.

'Cover me. They need help and fast.' With that, I slung the Sharps over my shoulder and clambered onto a pile of wooden crossties. Taking my life in my hands, I leapt from stack to stack. It was a precarious business, moving quickly over the various supplies, and one that wasn't aided by the constant movement of the flatbed cars.

Stopping to get my balance, I was just in time to see a warrior gallop to the side of the cab and literally fling himself on board, leaving his pony to its own devices. A firearm rang out inside, and the same figure was blasted back out of the cab, blood spurting from a chest wound. The fireman appeared brandishing a large horse pistol. Because of the increasingly fre-quent attacks, all the crews carried weapons. Aiming at another assailant, he fired, but the ball went wide.

Dan and Elijah were shooting continuously, but because of the sharp angle and the intervening cars theirs was not an easy task. Then one of the Sioux, controlling his pony entirely with his legs, snapped off a well-aimed shot that lifted the top off the fireman's head. As blood and brain matter splattered over the interior, the lifeless body tumbled from the cab. The horrific sight spurred me into action. If the engineer was also killed, then the whole supply train was in danger of running amok, because none of us had any idea of how to stop an engine. Once out of control, it would eventually plough into the railhead, slaughtering scores of workers . . . and us!

Scampering like a demented monkey across the piled supplies, I safely crossed another two cars, until only the coal tender lay between the engine and myself. The Sioux were well aware that the train was gathering speed, because they had to work their ponies harder to keep pace with it. Unwilling to risk certain death by boarding the cars under Dan and Elijah's guns, they made a last ditch attempt on the engine. A group of them drew level with it and unleashed a fusillade of arrows and bullets.

Throwing caution to the wind, I leapt across the gap between the last car and the tender, landing awkwardly on a pile of coal. Desperately struggling to keep my balance, I drew my Colt Navy Six just as the warriors urged their ponies over to the cab's entrance. Thumbing back the hammer, I fired again and again at the clutch of attackers, until eventually it struck on an empty chamber. Three riders were blasted from their animals, and the rest again veered away from the heavy fire. Unfortunately for them, this once more brought them in sight of my companions, and more gunfire reverberated over the plains.

Holstering my revolver, I bellowed out, 'I'm coming

in,' and then dropped down into the cab next to the startled engineer. He was a heavyset individual, coated in sweat and soot, and not a little blood.

'Are you hit?' I yelled over the noise of the engine, as I unslung my Sharps.

'Nah. Forehead creased by a ricochet, is all,' he answered dismissively. 'Them bastards couldn't hit a barn door with their new shooting irons.'

I sighed with relief. Now all I had to do was keep him alive. Cautiously poking the buffalo gun's muzzle out of the cab, I looked for a target. Joy filled my heart as I discovered that the attack was effectively over. With the smokestack belching soot, the train was beginning to outdistance the Sioux's tiring animals. We had done it. Huzzah!

Then something quite amazing took place. A lone Sioux warrior, raging at the unexpected turn of events, brutally urged his weary pony into a last ditch effort and charged directly at my two companions. With yet another stunning display of horsemanship, he controlled it with only his stocky legs. Working the lever-action of his Henry like a berserker, he fired bullet after bullet at the beleaguered white men. Although neither of them was able to rise up above their barricade of iron rails, they were not really in any immediate danger. How the warrior intended to capitalise on his momentary ascendancy would never be discovered, because at that moment I drew a fine bead on his mount and fired.

The pony's front legs buckled, pitching the brave

but foolhardy Indian over its head, and straight under the spinning wheels of the railroad cars. His gory demise was grotesque, but most likely instantaneous. Grimacing with distaste, I decided that I most certainly would not wish to be the one to carry out maintenance on that flat car's running gear!

And then, finally, it was all over. Accompanied by a triumphant blast on the steam whistle, the train left both the stampeding buffalo and the thwarted Sioux behind. Blowing out my cheeks like a horse, I turned away and began the laborious task of reloading my weapons. The Sharps was a matter of moments, but the cap 'n' ball Colt would be far more time consuming.

The engineer was regarding me intently. 'It's more than likely that you done saved my life, young fella.'

I couldn't disagree with him on that score, but before I had a chance to comment, he added, 'And just to show you how much I appreciate it, I've decided to make you my fireman.'

'What?' was all I could manage.

'I can't drive this great monster and feed the firebox as well.' Then he made a great show of peering around the cab, before smiling broadly. 'And there ain't no one else here but you!'

It occurred to me that he appeared to have got over the violent death of his fellow crewman remarkably quickly, but then I had no idea what sort of relationship they had enjoyed.

'Fair enough,' I replied. 'But you have to do something for me. When we get close to the railhead, I'll need you to stop this train so that I can have a parley with my companions. Savvy?'

'Now, why would you be wanting to do that, young fella?'

His slightly condescending manner was beginning to grate on me. Settling an unblinking gaze on him, I remarked, 'Because I've just said so. And I'm answerable only to God and General Dodge, so don't press me, old man!' By way of emphasize, I just happened to allow the muzzle of my Navy Six to nudge his ample stomach.

The engineer's eyes widened slightly, and he hurriedly nodded. 'No need to get your dander up, Mister. It's just my way, is all.' Then, to show that he wasn't completely cowed, he added, 'The shovel's over yonder.'

I nodded coolly. 'When I've recharged this Colt. It's saved your life once already, and may have to again, 'cause we ain't at the railhead yet.'

CHAPTER NINE

The sun was approaching its zenith when the supply train came to a temporary halt. Sweating like a plantation hand, I was immensely grateful to down tools for a while. I couldn't have imagined just how hot it could get in the cab, which 'benefited' from both the heat of the boiler and that radiating from the sun above. In addition to that, I had a relentlessly throbbing headache, presumably brought on by Elijah's blow to my face. Consequently, I was not in the best of moods as I advanced down the side of the flatbed cars. This was not improved when I clambered up to join my companions: whilst seeking to avoid the dried blood and flesh clinging to the running gear, I painfully stubbed a thumb on an iron rail.

What I saw upon reaching the two passengers was therefore only guaranteed to inflame me even more. Dan and our 'prisoner' were idly lounging in the midst of the supplies as though they hadn't got a care in the world. In truth there wasn't really anything to occupy them, but the sight of Elijah still in possession of a firearm infuriated me.

'For Christ's sake,' I barked at Dan, 'what's he doing still toting a gun?'

As Elijah stared at me sullenly, Dan registered both surprise and bewilderment. 'But what if we get jumped by some hostiles again?' he queried plaintively.

'Well, then you give it back to him,' I retorted angrily. 'He's lucky not to be still bound and gagged!' Without any warning, I abruptly aimed my Sharps at Elijah's belly. 'Hand it over to him!'

That man's features flushed red. 'You're a real ball breaker, ain't you? I helped fight off them savages, you know.' Nevertheless, he reluctantly passed the Spencer over to Dan.

What I did next came as an even bigger shock to him. Reaching out, I seized the Henry rifle from my friend and thrust it under Elijah's nose. 'You see this? If the damned army ever gets out here to protect us, they won't have anything as good. I took it off a dead Sioux warrior a few days ago. They'd just attacked the buffalo hunters that had taken over from us. And the redskin that's decorating the side of this rail car was using one against you. Don't you get it? You could have been killed by one of the same rifles sold by the son of a bitch you've been working for!'

As my angry words sank in, Elijah glanced at Dan, as though seeking confirmation. That man nodded grimly, his normally cheerful face completely devoid of any good humour.

'Yeah. Oh, yeah!' I roared at him. 'You might not like me any, but would you want Dan here to be spilling his guts out over the prairie just so your boss can get rich on blood money?'

Elijah switched his gaze back to me, and thought long and hard about that. Finally he replied, 'No, I guess not.'

I handed the Henry over to my friend, and began to thoughtfully massage my aching temple. 'So are you coming back to the railhead as my prisoner or as my employee?'

Not for the first time that day, Elijah's face registered surprise. It was obvious that the last thing he'd expected was to be offered another job. He didn't require quite so long to mull over that question. 'I reckon it'll have to be as your employee . . . once more. If you'll have me.'

'So, I'll ask you again. Who have you been working for?'

He appeared to be genuinely shamefaced at that. 'Nobody ever told me his name. His instructions just came through the fella whose throat you slit.'

Dismayed, I asked, 'So what do you know about him?'

'Real carriage trade. Leather shoes you could see your face in, and it seemed like his frockcoat had never been worn before. And he looked at me like I was a piece of hammered shit.'

It all sounded so familiar. 'Small, with a thin moustache?'

'Yeah, that's right,' Elijah proclaimed. 'Seems like you've already met him.'

'I have, once, but he didn't have a lot to say,' I murmured absentmindedly. Already I was pondering how Elijah's swapping sides could benefit us. Then it suddenly occurred to me. I glanced over at Dan and remarked, 'It's time for you to get your hands dirty. I've got other things to attend to. There's a shovel waiting for you in the cab.' Seeing his crestfallen expression, I smiled and added, 'You're getting off easy. We're nearly at the railhead.'

As Dan reluctantly scrambled off towards the sweatbox, I turned to my 'new' employee. 'I'm gonna need you to become my prisoner again . . . gag and all. The good part about it is that you'll now be getting five dollars a day and found. Life's looking up, huh?' Despite my throbbing head, I had to laugh out loud at his stunned expression.

Our arrival at the railhead created quite a stir. There was nothing unusual about a supply train pulling in, but this one had a car coated with blood and had acquired a new fireman en route. As I got to my feet amongst the iron rails, I could see Jack Casement's squat, muscular figure over by the engine. The track boss was in deep conversation with the engineer. I felt a sudden surge of affection for the familiar features. After days spent fending off various threats, it was good to be back amongst some friendly faces. Not that General Jack was always affable.

'What the hell have you been up to, Wakefield?' was his opening remark.

For some reason, I no longer felt quite so much in awe of him. Staring him straight in the eye, I replied, 'There's two things I want before we get to that. I need my prisoner locking up, and then I need to talk to you in private, where no one else can overhear.'

Obviously bemused, he tilted his head slightly. 'In case you hadn't noticed, Wakefield, this ain't some kind of army stockade. It's a railhead that's moving west all day, every day.'

'So chain him to a sleeper, or a rail. Who cares? Just don't harm him, is all. I need him. *We* need him!'

The other man took all this in, including my more noticeably forthright manner. 'OK. OK. I'll go along with this until I see how things pan out, but you've got some explaining to do.'

A short while later the two of us were standing face to face on the edge of camp, or leastways we would have been had he stood on a box. Any conversation would be drowned out by the constant noise of track laying and cussing. Dan had remained with the train, guarding the strongbox until our return.

Staring up at me, the track boss got started first. 'Before we get to it, I want to say that you did good on the journey out here. The engineer told me what happened. And I also got word of Cody's little shindig.

Seeing his wounded man, it appeared to me like you probably had more involvement than they gave you credit for.'

'Thank you,' I replied. 'That means a lot to me.' I paused to draw in a deep breath. I really hadn't been looking forward to this moment. 'Can I trust you, Mister Casement?'

He appeared to swell in size before my eyes. 'That's a hell of a thing to ask *me*, Wakefield. You'd better have a damn good reason to come up with a question like that!'

'Oh, I have. There's a crook working for the Union Pacific. He's high up. Maybe one of the directors.'

His response to that was not at all what I had expected. 'Hah. All the directors are crooks in their own way. Why do you think they're so rich?'

That momentarily floored me, but I hadn't finished with him yet. 'Crooked enough to be supplying Henry repeaters to the Sioux in exchange for the company's stolen gold?'

Now that *did* get his undivided attention. 'You mean the gold that General Dodge was talking about?'

'The very same. I know that because I've got it back. It's in a strongbox on the train, along with one of the rifles he's been peddling.'

'Sweet Jesus, you're full of surprises today,' he retorted.

'Oh, I haven't even got started yet. And this is where it gets kind of tricky. Who was the other man in the carriage that day, with the general? The short cuss with the moustache?'

'Why?'

I related the whole story, swiftly but with precision. From retrieving the Henry whilst helping out Bill Cody, to following and apprehending the Indian traders, then the steamboat disaster, and finally the deadly fracas in the Omaha livery. Some sixth sense told me to withhold the full truth about our 'prisoner'.

'Good God, I see it all now,' he exclaimed. At that moment, the walking boss called out to him from trackside, but Casement bellowed back, 'Not now, Shaughnessy!' Then his eyes were back on mine like limpets. 'So you think the chief engineer might be involved, don't you?'

'I don't know what to think. That's why I'm talking to you.'

Casement's mind seemed to drift off for long moments as he considered our predicament. He alternately chewed his top lip and scratched his hairy chin. I had never before seen him so preoccupied. A full five minutes passed before he returned his attention to me, and he seemed to have arrived at a judgment.

'I served under General Dodge in the war and I've worked for him since. Nothing that I've seen of him would have me believe him capable of being involved in such dark deeds. The other fella you described goes by the name of Oliver Dix. He's a director of the Union Pacific. I don't know anything about him, but I took agin him from the first time I met him. He looks like he could be a real awkward cuss, and dangerous.' He uttered a deep sigh. 'Hell, you've sure opened a real can of worms, Wakefield.'

'I've been doing what I was told to do . . . by General Dodge,' I replied.

He smiled his acknowledgement of that fact. 'Oh, that you have. And have you also considered what you'll do next?'

I quite liked that. The track boss himself was asking me. 'Well, actually, I have. The way I see it, you need to telegraph a message to Omaha for the sole attention of General Dodge, telling him we've recovered the gold, and a prisoner who's got a story to tell about where it's come from . . . if we can make him talk. And then we sit back and see what happens.'

Casement's eyes narrowed thoughtfully. 'That prisoner, I've seen him before somewhere.'

'He used to work for me as a skinner, until he was tempted away by easy money from the son of a bitch I'm after.' That wasn't strictly the whole truth, but it would suffice.

Amazingly, the track boss merely nodded his satisfaction. 'Seems like I've got a message to write. I just hope you can handle whatever comes of it.' And with that, he turned back towards the bustling railhead. As always, there were matters that required his attention.

I remained where I was for a moment to take in the sprawling vista of noisy activity. It seemed to me that whatever might happen, nothing would halt the laying of track, and in a way that was comforting. It made me feel as though I had returned to normality. The question was, how long would that last?

'I don't know why I have to stay chained up like this,' Elijah whined. 'I've already done told you I'm your man again.'

The three of us inhabited a surprisingly spacious tent, which my newly enhanced status apparently merited. It was also pitched well in advance of any working parties, so that we would have some privacy before the freshly laid track caught up with us at the close of the working day. Our 'prisoner' was secured to one of the sturdy support posts. In truth, I did feel a little sorry for him, but needs must.

'I reckon it won't just be supplies that arrive on the next train,' I answered obliquely.

Dan made no attempt to hide his confusion. 'What on earth can you mean by that?'

My response was tinged with cynicism. 'Just because Casement sent the telegraph message to General Dodge, doesn't mean it's him that gets to read it first.'

Now that really got Elijah's attention, and also proved that he was no fool. 'You mean I'm the bait, trussed up like a Thanksgiving turkey as I am?'

Glancing briefly at the strongbox sitting next to him, I shrugged apologetically. 'You and the gold both, but that's just the way it is. And besides, you called it when you turned outlaw!'

'Outlaw! I ain't no stinking outlaw. I just needed a

114

job, is all . . . after *you* gave me the heave ho! Come to think about it, you still owe me some *dinero* for skinning all them buffalo.'

This was getting us nowhere, and besides, if any of us were to survive the following day, I needed to come up with a plan, again. 'Keep an eye on things, Dan,' I remarked briskly, and ducked out of the tent.

'Oh, that's just great!' I heard Elijah exclaim, as I moved away.

Instinctively I gazed off to the east, back along the existing track to Omaha, my mind taking in, but not really processing the recently built siding. As yet, Casement apparently hadn't had a response to his telegraph . . . if indeed he had even sent one. I groaned. I was getting paranoid. I really had to work on the basis that he had, and therefore prepare for whatever came at us the following day.

Ignoring the curious glances of Shaughnessy and his tracklayers, I prowled around, weighing up my options. Obtaining a defensible position at a continuously mobile railhead would not be easy, yet there had to be a way. Because one thing was for sure, no amount of canvas would stop a bullet!

Then, suddenly, it all began to come together. Iron had stopped plenty of bullets on the way out from Omaha. I took in the construction train, which was closely shadowing the labourers. It contained rails, ties, sledgehammers and shovels; in fact, everything that could possibly be needed in the laying of a railroad. There was no way that Casement would let me interfere with that, but then I transferred my gaze to our supply train. By mid-afternoon that would be unloaded and heading back to its base, making way for the next train the following day. But what if it didn't go back? What if it was just moved onto the siding?

Turning all my attention to the familiar train, I took in the engine, tender and flat cars. With the rails and timber removed, the cars would no longer afford any protection at all. The cab, although solidly built, could be approached from both sides and behind. That left the high-sided tender, which was only really easily accessible from its front, where the fireman shovelled out the coal. With so much weight to haul, a great deal of that fuel had been consumed on the journey out, leaving a grimy yet potentially useable area.

For long moments I stared at the possible refuge, trying to decide whether I was losing my grip on reality. It seemed bizarre that in the midst of a vast, bustling railhead, my companions and I might find ourselves besieged by a gang of gun thugs. Then, recollecting our experience in Omaha, I decided that it was after all quite possible. The tracklayers were armed against attack by Indians. They were unlikely to be little more than curious at the attempts of fellow white men to apprehend some apparent fugitives. Any reaction from the workforce would depend very much on Jack Casement's role in all this, which inevitably brought me back to my biggest fear: could I really trust him?

*

'Are you out of your goddamn mind, Wakefield?' the track boss erupted. We were standing in his tent. A large map of Nebraska Territory was spread over a trestle table next to him. 'Do you realize what you're asking?'

I stared down at the much shorter man's belligerent features, and began to wonder whether there was more than just the prospect of disruption behind his anger. 'I know *exactly* what I'm asking. If there are men coming to do us harm, I want the three of us behind iron walls, and there's nothing else in this camp that will serve as well. *And* the Union Pacific has got plenty of trains. They ain't gonna miss one for a day or so. It just needs your say so, is all.'

Casement snorted loudly, before unexpectedly favouring me with the makings of a grin. 'You got grit, Wakefield. I'll give you that. OK, I'm persuaded. Just don't wreck the thing, *is all*. Tell the engineer to move it off the main line.' It was then that he displayed an unexpectedly softer side to his nature. 'Then he's got the rest of the day off. I hear tell he's taking the death of his partner hard. Give him my condolences.'

I returned his grin. 'Thank you, Mister Casement. I'm obliged. And I'll pass on your sentiments.'

As I turned to leave the tent, he caught me with one more question. 'Have you got anything out of that prisoner yet?'

'Not yet. I think he's hoping to be rescued.'

'Hmm. Happen it's time you started beating on him. If that ain't to your taste, I'm sure Shaughnessy will oblige. He's always been mighty free with his fists.'

'I'll think on it,' I replied. Then, just on the point of ducking through the flap, one more thing came to me. 'Do you keep any nitroglycerin in camp?'

The track boss regarded me strangely for a moment. 'For sure. The graders use it for blasting. It's mighty dangerous stuff. Why?'

Without directly answering, I replied, 'I could use a bottle or two. Strictly for medicinal purposes, of course.'

His eyes widened expressively at such a preposterous comment, but he nevertheless nodded. 'Why the hell not? You're getting everything else today. You must have caught me in a good mood.'

I was definitely tempting fate. It was time to leave and so, flipping him a cheery salute, I did just that. As I walked off, I couldn't resist a quiet chuckle at the thought of Elijah's reaction to the prospect of a visit from the hulking walking boss.

The engineer greeted the surprising news of his delayed departure with huge relief. 'Never thought I'd be getting considerations from General Jack,' he declared, his voice slightly slurred.

I had caught him in his cab, supping out of an earthenware jug, and from the anguished expression on his face he had doubtless been reliving that morning's gruelling experience. His earlier apparent detachment over the fireman's slaying had obviously been due to the heat of the moment, because there were tears coursing down his ruddy cheeks. Although embarrassed at disturbing him, I nevertheless had more to impart.

'I need you to move this train onto the siding . . . *before* you drink any more. Savvy? If you don't, you'll answer to the Jack Casement that you're more used to dealing with!'

That definitely sank in. He nodded hurriedly, and staggered to his feet.

'One more thing,' I added gently. 'Where will you be if I need you?'

'Somewhere's about,' he mumbled. 'I sure won't be straying far, what with those heathen devils on the loose.'

Deciding that such a commitment was the best that I could expect under the circumstances, I left him to his task and returned to my companions.

'Sweet Jesus! You can't intend for the three of us to spend the whole night in a coal tender,' Elijah exclaimed.

'No. No, I don't,' I replied. 'The supply train won't arrive until late morning. So we'll eat our fill, courtesy of the railroad, and then get a good night's shuteye. Dan and I deserve it after you and your cronies rousted us out last night!'

Talk of food perked up the prisoner. 'It's about time. My belly was beginning to think my throat had been slit.' Then he seemed to recall the way in which I had killed a man the previous night, because his eyes grew guarded, and he coloured slightly. 'Never took you for a knife fighter, Joe. You always shied away from cutting up buffalo.'

I shrugged. 'That's because I had you two to do the work for me. Knife work's messy and ugly, but if I'm pushed I'll do what I need to. You'd do well to remember that.'

For a long moment our eyes remained locked, until Dan broke the spell. 'If you two have finished eye-balling each other, let's go eat. He ain't the only cuss that's famished.'

I smiled at him. 'Fair enough, but we go in shifts. And he stays here.'

'Whaaat?' Elijah exclaimed unhappily.

I gestured in the direction of the tracklayers. 'Casement thinks you need roughing up some, and there's a massive Irish walking boss over yonder who's up for the job. So it's best that you stay out of sight.' As the colour visibly left Elijah's face, I added, 'You go first, Dan. And bring back a plateful for our guest here. Pile it high. He looks like he could use it.'

Coincidentally, as Dan departed, the construction engine's whistle blew for time, and the day's work ended abruptly. As planned when the tent had been pitched, we were now directly opposite the railhead, but wouldn't have to suffer the incessant din, because the famished men would soon be heading for the long benches in the dining car, and then some well-earned rest. As relative quiet descended on the temporarily static camp, I hunkered down next to Elijah and removed his chains.

'Don't make me regret doing this,' I remarked. As he ruefully rubbed his wrists, I continued, 'The cockchafer that employed you in Omaha goes by the name of Oliver Dix. He's a big noise with the railroad. If push comes to shove, how many gun thugs can he call on?'

The other man shook his head in apparent frustration. 'There really ain't a whole lot more I can tell you, Joe. After you and me had words, I went back there looking for work, any kind of work that paid cash money. I rubbed up against the fella you ventilated in one of the saloons, and before I knew it I had a grubstake and a berth in some flophouse. It seemed like easy living to me . . . until we ran into you at the livery. If he's got money, this Dix could buy any number of hired guns. Place like Omaha attracts plenty of drifters.'

'Hmm.' I was disappointed at the lack of clarity, but not in the least bit surprised. 'Well, it looks like we'll just have to wait and see who turns up on the supply train tomorrow then, don't it?'

Elijah nodded solemnly.

'Just don't let me down, is all,' I added earnestly. 'When you side with a man, you stick with him. Otherwise you're no better than some animal!'

121

CHAPTER TEN

The horny hand over my mouth seemed intent on choking me, and although fogged with sleep my natural instinct was to fight back. I began to twist and buck until a familiar voice penetrated my disorientation.

'For God's sake, wake up, Josiah. It's me, Dan.'

With my heart thumping like an anvil strike, I peered through the gloom in the tent. 'What is it? What's wrong?' I finally managed.

'There's a train pulling in. Now. This very minute!'

Suddenly wide-awake, I stayed still and listened. It required little effort. The hissing of steam. The sound of metal on metal. All too familiar noises that were occurring exactly when they shouldn't be. My first thought was that it was our engineer, disobeying orders and heading back to Omaha. Except for one little thing . . . the sounds were coming closer.

It was Elijah, fully conscious and lucid, who clarified our fears. 'That telegram got sent all right. And now someone's coming for you . . . us. And they must have some pull, to get a special train.'

I knew that he was correct. I also knew that we couldn't remain in the tent. Thrusting the Henry at Elijah, I commanded, 'You two, grab the strongbox and make for the tender. I'm going to see just what we're up against. If I start shooting, give 'em hell. But just be careful, huh?' They both knew exactly what I meant by that!

Conveniently, the flap of the large tent faced away from the main track. I had no idea what time it was, but there was no sign that daybreak was in the offing. As my companions scurried away with their horde of Double Eagles, I dropped onto all fours. With the Sharps in the crook of my arm, I crawled around the side of the tent. An amazing sight greeted my eyes.

A great Iron Horse, illuminated by an unusual number of kerosene lamps, was grinding to a halt in the midst of the encampment. The railhead's night guards, drawn by the unexpected arrival, approached the manmade beast cautiously. They attempted to shield their eyes against the bright light, but were already losing their night vision. I, on the other hand, kept one eye tightly closed.

As the machine finally came to a stop, I was able to make out the single carriage behind it. No supply cars of any kind, just one solitary passenger car. I cursed under my breath. I had been a fool, expecting our enemies to stick to a timetable when they were after a fortune in gold!

Dim shapes began to appear on the outside platform at the front of the carriage. And they kept on coming. Some dropped down onto either side of the track, and they all carried long guns.

'Just who the hell are you, fellas?' a night guard called out, as he approached them warily with his weapon cocked.

'We're here on railroad business,' boomed a loud voice on the platform.

'Well, so are we,' the guard retorted petulantly. 'And we were here first.'

Good for you, I thought approvingly. It had occurred to me immediately that the new arrivals were obviously overconfident of their numbers to be making so much noise. Their swelling ranks did seem to have an effect on the guard though, because his belligerence wasn't to last long.

'You'd be wise to back off and save your smart remarks for the goddamn Sioux,' the imposing voice continued. 'We're here to apprehend two . . . maybe three fugitives. They've stolen a company strongbox, and killed many men.'

Even in the gloom, it was apparent from his movements that the guard was beginning to view the dozen or so heavily armed men with some trepidation. 'Don't rightly know what "apprehend" means,' he responded. 'But I guess Mister Casement is the fella to sort all this out. He's in that big tent over yonder. I'd tread carefully, if I was you. He can be a mite prickly.'

The individual, whose face I still couldn't see,

grunted as though unimpressed and waved to his waiting men. Then, dropping down to trackside, he joined them, and together they all advanced on Casement's tent. Now we would definitely find out whose side that man was on!

Taking advantage of their temporary distraction, I moved away stealthily from our temporary abode. After making sure that I remained well clear of Dan and Elijah's line of fire, I dropped onto the grass again. I well knew that men were going to die that night, and that I might be one of them, but I felt strangely calm. Just like on the day that I killed my first Sioux warrior at the railhead. In reality mere days ago, but it felt like a lifetime had passed.

I wasn't kept waiting long. After maybe five minutes, the shadowy group re-emerged and headed directly for our tent! 'The bastard!' I snarled.

Pulling back the hammer of my Sharps, I took aim at the mass of men. The fact that it was still dark wouldn't hamper my effectiveness. Overconfident of their numbers, they had neglected to spread out, and now it would cost them dear. As my buffalo gun belched death, the relative calm of the night was shattered. One man collapsed, and before the others could scatter, my companions opened fire. Over by the tender, muzzle flashes momentarily flared in the dark.

As I rolled sideways and then reloaded rapidly, the bizarre thought struck me that any Sioux war party lurking out on the plains would likely be mighty puzzled by this turn of events.

As two more broken bodies tumbled to the ground, the survivors recalled some basic rules of combat, and scattered. With frantic speed, they fanned out in a defensive arc and went to ground. All that could be heard were the intermittent screams of one of their comrades.

'You're gonna regret this, you sons of bitches!' their leader bawled out.

I remained silent, so as not to give away my position, but not so Dan. 'Maybe, maybe not, you cockchafer, but right now you're the ones doing the screaming.'

That drew a predictable response. A fusillade of shots crashed out, merging with the tremendous din of hot lead striking the iron tender. I fired at a muzzle flash, and then rolled off to my right, putting yet more distance between our assailants and myself. I had a very good reason for doing so.

'You pus weasels'll have to do better than that,' Dan taunted, but this time the reaction was far more subdued. The new arrivals merely shifted position and held their fire.

Then, from one of the boxcars on the main line, Shaughnessy's very distinctive voice sounded off. 'The devil take it! What are you bastards after doing?'

The gang leader gave him short shrift. 'Keep out of this, Irish. We're on company business, and we've cleared it with your boss. This'll all be over soon, an' you can all go back to sleeping like babies.'

The walking boss was clearly not impressed, but he

did stay put. 'Sure, an' you're a fine man for thinking of us. *Póg mo thóin!*'

The prone gun thugs completely ignored that, and instead began whispering amongst themselves. I knew what that must be a prelude to. They had been caught by surprise, but still had a large superiority of numbers and could only be planning to rush our train.

It was then that I hollered out a pre-arranged warning that could hardly have any meaning to our attackers. 'Grenadiers ready!'

I again rolled sideways, but no lead came my way. The men were otherwise occupied. I held my breath Unconsciously. This was the tipping point, when it would either go our way or theirs.

'Now!' the gang leader hissed, and suddenly ten wraith-like figures were on their feet and moving rapidly towards the tender.

With my eyes closed in readiness, I had no chance of seeing the two bottles of nitroglycerin fly through the air, but the ensuing explosions shook the very ground that I lay on. Two blinding flashes momentarily turned night into day, and a buffeting shock wave blew over me. By Christ, that stuff had some power to it!

Opening my right eye, I swiftly took aim at a swaying form and fired. I must have hit it, because it disappeared from sight, and then my companions again opened fire. The dimly lit railhead was filled with detonations, muzzle flashes and the screams of the wounded. At no point had any of the gun thugs actually fired back. Our victory appeared to be complete.

Getting to my feet cautiously, I drew my Colt and advanced. 'Hold fire, boys,' I called at the tender.

Where the two explosions had occurred, wisps of smoke seemed to cling to the long grass, lending a strangely ethereal feel to the killing ground. And yet there was nothing otherworldly about the screams that emanated from one survivor. Despite the agony assailing him, his heightened senses seemed to discern my approach, and he called out, 'Kill me, Mister. For Christ's sake, just kill me!'

As I closed in, even the gloom and lingering smoke couldn't conceal the terrible burns to his face. I had seen such sights before, in the late war, but that didn't make them any easier to stomach. As his pitiful wailing reached a crescendo, I drew a bead on his skull and fired. The pathetic noise ceased immediately, leaving only hissing steam from the recently arrived train to break the peace.

'You OK over there, Josiah?' Dan queried anxiously.

'Reckon I'm the only one who is,' I retorted. 'Damn, but that nitro's deadly stuff.'

It was hard to believe that there were hundreds of men at the railhead, because at that moment it seemed as though we were the only ones left alive on the plains. It was as though a stunned silence had settled over the camp. Then a number of things happened at once. From beyond the perimeter came the rattling of a wagon, accompanied by the sound of pounding hoofs. I had a shrewd idea of who that would be, but chose to ignore it. Anger was building inside me. Anger that someone's greed and dishonesty was the cause of so much killing. I knew there and then what I had to do, but first I had a reckoning of another kind.

'Dan, Elijah, get the strongbox over to the train.'

'Which one?' Dan was obviously struggling to handle the speed of events.

'The one with steam up, of course,' I barked. 'And don't take any lip from the crew. Their shift's not over yet.'

Elijah spoke next. 'And where the hell are you going?'

'To have words with Mister Casement. There's something needs settling.' So saying, I holstered my Colt and hastily reloaded the Sharps.

As I strode towards the track boss's tent, Shaughnessy's great bulk suddenly appeared by his boxcar. 'Just what de hell are you after doing then, boyo?'

'This is no concern of yours, Shaughnessy,' I retorted. 'I've got business elsewhere, so don't try and stop me. You might be the very devil with your fists, but this .52 calibre rifle has more than got your measure. When this is all over, General Dodge himself will set you straight. I promise you.' The way things were shaping up, that seemed like one hell of a commitment, but mention of the chief engineer seemed to provide some small measure of reassurance to the walking boss. He didn't back off, but neither did he push his challenge any further.

As Bill Cody led his skinning team into camp noisily, I stalked over to Casement's tent and launched my self through the flap. General Jack stood, large as life, next to his portable cot. He had an oil lamp trimmed low, as though he had been expecting my arrival. His expression had lost none of its habitual belligerence, but what happened next took even him by surprise.

'You set us up, you bastard!' I snarled, slamming the Sharps' stock solidly into his midriff.

Immensely strong though he was, it was too much even for him to withstand. Doubling over in pain, he staggered back. I was ready to hit him again, but some vestige of restraint stopped me. Instead I waited for him to catch his breath.

'I did nothing of the kind, you stupid shit,' he finally managed.

'You sent them straight to our tent,' I accused.

'Yes, knowing that you wouldn't be there. And even if you had been, it would have made no never mind, because I'll tell you this, Wakefield. I ain't taking a bullet for any man!'

After all that I'd been through, that was too much to take. 'The hell with you and your goddamn railhead,' I retorted, and lashed out with my Sharps again.

This time Casement collapsed to his knees, and it was at that instant that I heard movement behind me. Twisting around, I backed up against the tent's canvas wall. Somehow I had known that 'Buffalo' Bill wouldn't

130

be able to keep his nose out of this, and he hadn't disappointed. The buckskin-clad figure stood just inside the entrance, his Sharps carbine pointing vaguely in my direction.

'My, my, my,' he remarked softly. 'This is one hell of an entertaining scene. I never thought to see anyone take a swing at the mighty track boss.'

'What brings you back in the dead of night?' I enquired suspiciously.

'I heard a noise!'

I sighed. I had neither the time nor inclination to bandy words with this man, but the muzzle of his gun dictated the need for a certain amount of caution. 'We had words over something that doesn't concern you.'

Tilting his head slightly, Cody favoured me with a toothy grin that failed to reach his suddenly steely eyes. 'You forget, I work for Mister Casement as well. How would it look if I just stood by and let you beat seven shades of shit out of him?'

'I've done what I came to do,' I explained patiently. 'And now, as I've just informed Shaughnessy, I have business elsewhere. Don't make this into something it doesn't need to be.'

'Such as?'

'You and me trading lead!'

It can't have escaped his notice that my own Sharps was held ready, and for a long moment we eyeballed each other steadily. I couldn't say with any certainty what might have happened, but mercifully the impasse was broken by Casement drawing air into his lungs. Grasping the table, he staggered to his feet.

'Leave it be, Cody. You're here to kill buffalo and nothing else. What happened in this tent stays in this tent. At least until Wakefield has done what he has to do in Omaha.' Slowly, he got to his feet and then glared at me. 'Get out of here before I change my mind. If I find out you've hoodwinked me, there'll be hell to pay!'

I needed no further encouragement. Easing cautiously past Cody, I left the tent and headed straight for the special train. With the whole camp now up and about, I was very conscious of a great many eyes following me, but mercifully no one attempted to rein me in. Reaching the hissing engine, I glanced up at the cab and found Dan's cheerful face watching me with obvious relief.

'I was grievously afeared we might not see you again, Josiah,' he remarked with obviously genuine feeling. 'Without you, we'd have been stopped in our tracks.'

I chuckled. The pun had completely escaped him, but who the hell cared? I was just damn glad to see him. Heaving myself up into the cab, I patted him affectionately on the back. 'Where's the box?'

'In the carriage with Elijah.' Seeing my instinctive alarm, he added, 'Don't fret yourself. He couldn't get far toting that weight by himself . . . and besides, these two fellas needed a little persuading.'

Glancing at the two grubby crewmen in the light of the firebox, I noticed that one of them sported a livid bruise on the side of his face. Grunting my approval, I remarked, 'Seems like Dan has already shown you our bona fides, so I'll keep this short. We're returning to Omaha . . . now. No arguments, no parley. Just get this thing moving!'

The engineer, who had already suffered my companion's wrath, glared at me briefly before nodding at the fireman. With the boiler still hot, it took no time at all to get us rolling out of the camp. Then, despite everything, he just couldn't contain himself. 'Is every single one of them gunhands dead?'

I jerked abruptly with surprise, because it was only now that it truly registered with me what we had just done. 'I . . . I guess they must be,' I stammered. 'Leastways none of them were moving. I can't answer for them now.'

The other man shook his head in horrified wonder. 'Well if that don't beat all,' he muttered. 'You fellas must be real dangerous men!' Then, as though coming to a decision, he stared sharply at me. 'There's one thing you do need to think on, mister. Come morning, there'll be another supply train heading this way . . . on the same and only track. So unless you've got a death wish, you're gonna have to pull off some pretty fancy moves!'

CHAPTER ELEVEN

It was still dark when I pulled the first of my moves. Once beyond audible range of the railhead, I glanced over at the engineer. Although the cab was rather crowded with four men occupying it, neither of the crewmen had said a word.

'What's your name?' I demanded.

His expression was sullen, but he knew better than to ignore me. 'Zachary.'

'Well, Zachary, I want you to stop this thing right next to a telegraph pole, so that light from one of these lamps shines on it. Savvy?'

His sweaty features now registered both surprise and annoyance. 'I don't know what you're fixing on doing, Mister, but I just got to set you right on one little matter.' Caressing the control tenderly under his right hand, he suddenly stated with surprising passion, 'This ain't a thing. She's a fine piece of precision engineering, an' unlike a woman, if you treat her right she'll never let you down!'

I stared long and hard at him, until he began to pale visibly. Then I uttered a deep sigh. So much had been going through my mind that it had only just dawned on me: just because this train had delivered a gang of assassins to the railhead, didn't mean that these two men were involved. They were more than likely just ordinary employees, called upon to crew a very unusual train.

'You're quite right, and I'm sorry,' I blurted out abruptly. 'Sorry about your face, as well. If I survive all this, the Union Pacific will make it up to you. You have my word on it.'

His tired eyes widened in surprise. An apology was obviously the last thing that he had expected. 'Yeah, well, OK I guess.' He paused, as though mulling something over. 'Perhaps if you were to tell me a little of what you're up to, so that I understood, then I might be able to help you survive.'

I could see everything to gain and nothing to lose by it, so I did just that.

'Hot dang,' he finally opined. 'You fellas sure have been busy.'

'Far too busy for some. That's why I need to stop anyone at the railhead telegraphing Omaha about us. This cuss Dix won't be expecting us to turn up on his own train, and I need to keep it that way.'

With a now fully cooperative engineer in charge, the train ground to a halt on the darkened track in exactly the right spot. Light from a kerosene lamp illuminated the Western Union's telegraph line. Even so, it would be a difficult shot. High up on the pole, and set well back from the track, the thin wire was only barely visible.

'Go join Elijah in the carriage, Dan. It doesn't need two of us in here. And tell him not to worry about the shooting.' With that I cocked and levelled my Sharps.

As my friend, who was never in any doubt as to the probable success of my shot, dropped down to trackside, I took careful aim at the modern marvel of communication. It suddenly occurred to me that the last time a white man had maliciously severed a telegraph line would likely have been in the war. Smiling grimly, I held my breath and fired, and was immediately rewarded by a metallic twang, as the taut wire snapped.

'Hell, but that was fine shooting, mister,' Zachary remarked appreciatively. 'Were you in the late conflict, by any chance?'

'Berdan's Sharpshooters.'

'I knew it. You've got the look.'

'I've also got a fine weapon with honest sights,' I responded. Then, after blowing powder residue out of the breech, I added, 'Right, mister engineer, let's move 'em out, if you please. The sooner we get to Omaha, the sooner you can get your head down.'

It was full daylight by the time I made my next move, only this time it wasn't of my doing. Since my act of

136

sabotage, I had spent the intervening hours alternately dozing on the floor of the cab, and scheming. So it was actually Zachary who instigated the action because, as I well knew, he too had been doing plenty of thinking. The engineer comprehended only too well what was coming directly for us.

'Supply train'll be on its way,' he bellowed out over the engine noise. 'I reckon we should pull into the next siding.'

I grinned up at him. He might not have enjoyed having his train commandeered, but he sure as hell didn't want to die in it. 'Sounds good to me. Just don't try to make any *unnecessary* contact with the other train as it passes. Savvy?'

The older man returned the grin. 'I understand. And it's time for you to put in some more effort. There just happens to be a siding up ahead, an' you'll have to change the points.'

These extra lengths of parallel track had been periodically constructed near the railhead to allow for the manoeuvrings of supply trains, and had been left in place. As our train came to a halt, I dropped down from the cab and seized hold of the heavy control lever. It took a great deal of effort, but gradually it swung over its 180 degree arc, so changing the direction of the track.

'I'm surprised you didn't tell me to do it,' Dan bawled from the passenger carriage. 'I usually get all the shit jobs!'

With remarkable ease, our train swung onto the

other track, and I returned the lever to its original position. 'You'll get your chance,' I called over, before scampering back to the engine. I had just seen a plume of smoke approaching from the east. Damn, but we'd cut it fine.

Back in the cab, I glanced over at Zachary. 'It might help if you gave him a friendly wave on his way past,' I suggested.

The fireman, who until that point hadn't uttered a word, noisily snorted. 'You expect a lot, mister. Considering you done kidnapped us!'

Surprisingly, it was his partner who came back at him. 'Hush, Lemual. He's only doing his job. And it sure ain't one I could handle.'

The heavily laden supply train, a mirror image of the one we had occupied the previous day, chugged steadily past. The engineer stared curiously at us, but Zachary favoured him with a cheery salute and the thumbs up sign. It seemed to do the trick, because they didn't even slow down.

'He wouldn't have pulled up without sound reason,' Zachary explained. 'Not with the Sioux on the loose like they are.'

'You did good,' I remarked emphatically, before bellowing back to Dan to inform him that his turn on the points had come. 'And now, since we ain't gonna have a head on collision anymore, how's about taking us to Omaha?' Before he could answer, I added, 'It might interest you to know that if we had had one, it sure wouldn't have been the first this week!'

*

It was barely mid-morning when the city's rooftops came into view. Our lightly laden train had made good time.

'Slow up here,' I ordered. 'Just long enough for me to move into the carriage.' Impulsively, I reached out to shake Zachary's hand. 'And thanks.'

He accepted my grasp and winked. 'As soon as we stop near the engine sheds, you won't see us for dust. Whatever's coming your way, we don't want any part of it. Fair enough?'

'Fair enough,' I agreed.

As the train slowed to a crawl, I leapt down and raced for the carriage. As soon as I gained the platform, it then picked up speed again. Both men were surprised to see me.

'Can those two be trusted on their own?' Elijah demanded.

'I reckon so. They've no love for the bosses, and they certainly don't want to be around more gunplay.'

'And where do we stand now?' Dan asked. 'Apart from up shit creek without a paddle.'

I regarded my two companions with what I hoped was outward calm. 'We're staying right here to wait on events.'

Elijah shook his head in dismay. 'Ain't that just inviting trouble?'

'Maybe,' I allowed. 'But you can bet that Dix will hear of this train's arrival immediately. And since he'll think it's full of his own men, I believe he'll come to collect this gold in person.' Glancing through the nearest window towards town, I continued. 'So let's give him something to ponder. Pull down all these blinds, and then get the strongbox over to the door.'

With just the one blind left marginally raised, and with me stationed behind it as lookout, we then settled down to wait. I managed a fleeting smile at the sight of our crewmen beating a hasty retreat, but after that time weighed heavy on me. There were plenty of Union Pacific employees working nearby, but strangely no one approached the new arrival. It was almost as though they knew to keep clear of it.

Thankfully, it wasn't long before there was some meaningful activity. A spacious open carriage, drawn by two well-groomed horses, swept out towards the tracks. Two men rode in it, and a third followed on horseback. Even keeping back from the window, so as not to be seen through the inch or two of raised blind, I easily recognized the immaculate figure of Oliver Dix.

The carriage came to a halt close by, and the outrider drew level with them. Together, for a long moment, they all peered expectantly at the surprisingly quiet railway car. Then Dix nodded impatiently at the horseman, and that man bellowed out, 'You in there. There'll be time enough for sleeping later. Get yourselves out here, now!'

When nothing at all happened, Dix glanced at the minion next to him. 'This is the damnedest thing.

Don't they realize who's waiting on them? Get in there and roust them out. If they've been drinking, it'll cost them dear!'

That man clambered out of the carriage and approached the steps to the platform. Taking a fleeting look at Dan, I made a clubbing gesture with my Sharps, and he nodded.

Despite his obvious desire to appear detached from the doings of lesser mortals, Dix obviously couldn't completely contain his anticipation, because he too alighted the carriage.

Leather boots thudded up onto the platform, and the door was flung open abruptly, flooding the interior with light. As I had envisaged, the man's eyes fastened on to the strongbox alone. An avaricious smile spread across his seedy features, and he moved forward eagerly.

Without any warning, the Spencer's iron butt smashed into the side of his skull, and he went down as though pole-axed. Dix heard the heavy thump, but with his thoughts presumably consumed by greed, he wasn't alarmed by it immediately. Not so his mounted subordinate. 'Something ain't right here, boss,' he announced, drawing a massive Le Mat revolver from his belt.

Not at all keen to chance the twenty-gauge shotgun charge that it contained, I thrust my Sharps through the window. 'Don't even think about cocking that piece,' I warned. 'Or you'll join your *compadres* at the railhead!'

141

His hand froze, but not so his mouth. 'What kind of threat's that?'

'A mighty good one. They're all paroled to Jesus,' I replied, by way of enlightenment. 'Every mother's son of them.'

The gun thug paled, but his employer apparently could still think only of Double Eagles. 'Who the devil is in there? Show yourself immediately!'

Without taking my eyes of the horseman, I remarked to my companions, 'I think he *really* wants that box. Guess you'd better give it to him.'

Dan was astounded. 'What are you saying?'

'I'm saying, *really* give it to him. Into his lap. Savvy?'

Oh, they savvied, all right. Chuckling together, like two juvenile conspirators, they both picked up the extremely heavy strongbox and lugged it out onto the platform.

'Who the hell are you two?' Dix demanded.

'Ain't he just the dandy?' Elijah put to Dan.

'And then some,' Dan replied, and together they tossed the box full of gold coins at the feet of the uncomprehending Oliver Dix.

Out of my peripheral vision, I saw it land squarely on his highly polished boots. Abruptly screaming with pain, his reserved demeanour changed to one of total anguish. Doubling over, he tried desperately to heave it off, but couldn't summon the strength.

'Keep that other cuss covered,' I called to the others, before scooting through the carriage and on to the platform. Dix regarded me through pain-wracked eyes, and surprise momentarily overcame distress.

'*You*!'

I nodded grimly. 'The very same. You wanted the gold that bad. Now you've got it!'

His no doubt habitual arrogance had completely dissipated. 'Please, just get this off me!'

I had other ideas. 'First, you've got to tell me where we can find General Dodge. You and I are going to go visit with him together.'

'Whaaat?'

'You heard me,' I barked. 'Where is the Union Pacific's chief engineer? We've got a lot to talk about.'

The pain had grown too great. Moaning piteously, he collapsed onto his backside, with the front of his feet still trapped under the great weight. Whatever fears had suddenly beset him, they were nothing to the stabbing agony.

'He's in the Cozzens House Hotel on 9th and Harney.' In spite of everything, he couldn't resist adding, 'It's the best they've got in this shithole. Not that you're likely to know.'

'I'm about to find out,' I responded bleakly, before glancing at my companions. 'Release this little turd, and check him for pocket cannons and the like.' Then, swinging my Sharps over to cover the motionless horseman, I ordered, 'You, get down off of that horse. Real slow, like molasses in the wintertime.'

As the gun thug complied, I moved over to him, ignoring the agonised groaning on my left. 'Now, place that piece on the ground in front of you,

143

keeping your finger well clear of the trigger.'

He was a big, long-legged fellow, which meant that as his revolver touched the ground, his upper body was parallel to it. At that moment I stepped forward, and swung the Sharps in a great roundhouse sweep so that the stock struck his head with sickening force. He toppled sideways and landed in a heap next to his large belt gun.

'Holy shit, you sure lit into him,' Dan remarked.

Gazing reflectively at the LeMat, I replied, 'It was mostly Johnny Rebs that toted these things, so happen he got what he deserved.' With that, I returned my full attention to Oliver Dix. He gripped his right foot, whilst emitting a pitiful keening sound.

'You better quit that blubbering,' I rasped. 'You done started all of this, an' now you're gonna answer for it.'

In spite of his anguish, the dapper crook still managed to compose a retort. 'It was those painted savages that caused all this by stealing the gold in the first place.' Then a spasm of pain shot though his foot, and he cried out, 'You've broken my toes, you ignorant bastard!'

After what we had all been through, that was not necessarily the most tactful remark. Bristling with anger, I retorted, 'I reckon the Sioux are a darn sight more noble than you, bringing death to your own people! Get him and the gold into that buggy, boys. We're taking a short ride.'

Dix was aghast. 'You're all madmen!'

144

'It kind of looks that way, don't it, *Mister* Dix?' Elijah commented. 'You don't remember me, do you?'

The railroad director regarded him with the same disdain as something he might wipe off his boot.

'No, I didn't think you would,' Elijah continued. 'I'm one of the hired guns you sent out looking for Joe here. Dodge should be right interested in my testimony.'

Suddenly it wasn't just great pain afflicting Dix. His mask of innate superiority was beginning to slip. That process was encouraged further by the discovery of a single barrelled Derringer in his trousers pocket. 'Happen you're a cardsharp as well, eh?' I muttered.

With Dan taking the reins, I squeezed onto the bench seat with our squirming prisoner wedged between us. Beneath us lay the strongbox.

As we rolled towards the hotel, with Elijah following on horseback, I delved abruptly into the pockets of Dix's frockcoat. This time it wasn't concealed weapons that concerned me, and what I found in an inner one answered a lot of questions.

'Unhand me, you damned scoundrel!' he exploded, but it was too late.

There, clenched between my fingers, was a transcript of the telegram that Casement had apparently sent for the sole attention of General Dodge, telling of our arrival at the railhead with the strongbox. Seemingly, the recipient had never received it.

Grabbing Dix by the throat, I squeezed . . . hard. 'When this is all over, little man, I'm gonna nail your

145

hide to the livery door,' I snarled. Only very reluctantly, did I finally release him, and by that time his complexion had turned purple.

CHAPTER TWELVE

The Cozzens House Hotel was the largest and easily the most splendid establishment of its kind anywhere on the frontier. And it only existed in Omaha because of the arrival of the Union Pacific Railroad. Frame-built and three storeys high, it could boast of one hundred and twenty rooms. It was the natural place to find General Dodge when he was in town.

The lobby staff were doubtless used to Mister Dix's comings and goings, but never in the circumstances that they now saw him. The four of us burst upon the splendid opulence, and ignoring the astonished glances, made straight for the stairs. Dan and Elijah toted the strongbox, whilst I none too gently manhandled the badly limping director. He was no longer his immaculate self, and we three Indian fighters were excessively grubby and foul smelling.

'Should we fetch the marshal, Mister Dix?' one of the employees called out nervously.

It was immediately obvious that that was the last

thing he required. 'No. Hell no!' he yelled back, spittle flying from his lips.

'Hot dang, I ain't never seen a hotel like this,' Dan panted, as he helped carry the gold up the wide stairs. 'How many's it sleep to a room?'

'I don't think it quite works like that, you numb-skull,' Elijah retorted.

And then we were there, in front of the room number that we had prised out of Dix. As I was about to knock on the door, something occurred to me. What if it was a ruse, and more of his thugs were in there? Cocking and adjusting the hammer of the LeMat, so that it would detonate the shotgun charge, I whispered to Dan, 'Kick that door in, then step aside.'

With my left hand gripping our trembling prisoner by the neck, I was all set. There was a great splintering crash, as the door gave way under Dan's boot. Propelling Dix before me as a shield, we surged into the room, my massive revolver ready for any threat. Yet there were no heavily armed pistoleros awaiting us, only the much-alarmed figure of General Dodge. He was ensconced behind a highly polished mahogany desk; it was very similar to the one I had seen in his railroad carriage. The room appeared to form part of a two-room suite, which entirely befitted a man of his status.

'What the hell is the meaning of . . . *Oliver*!' Initially only aware of three unknown characters behind his dishevelled colleague, Dodge instinctively reached towards a desk drawer. Then he saw my face, and his hand froze. 'I know you. You're Casement's man. The Indian fighter.'

'That's right, General. Joe Wakefield at your service.'

His sharp eyes took in my various weapons. 'You appear to be loaded for bear, Mister Wakefield.'

I relaxed slightly, and lowered my revolver. 'It's not all I'm loaded with. Put it next to his desk, boys.'

My two companions did just that, and then with a flourish, Dan produced his skinning knife. Dodge's bearded features again registered alarm, which changed to curiosity as the honed blade sliced through the tightly bound rawhide securing the strongbox. Curiosity then turned to disbelief, as the lid was pulled back to reveal the horde of gleaming gold coins. The new day was unexpectedly providing the chief engineer with a full gamut of emotions. So much so that he still hadn't even queried the reason for his colleague's distress.

'Well I'll be a . . . the missing payroll,' he exclaimed, jumping to his feet to get a better look. 'How did you get your hands on this? And why are you treating Mister Dix like a felon?'

Releasing my grip on that individual, I pushed him to one side contemptuously. 'Because it's all he deserves. Him and the gold are very much connected, General.' I then, briefly but precisely, related to him everything of relevance since our last meeting in his railroad carriage.

'Everything he's just told you about me is a damned lie, Grenville,' Dix remarked angrily from his new position on the polished timber floor. His broken foot could no longer support his weight, and he was obviously in a great deal of pain, but his mind was as sharp as ever. 'Next he'll be saying that it was me stole the gold in the first place.'

Dodge had dropped back into his chair whilst I spoke, and now sat deep in thought, giving no sign of even having heard Dix's protests. I had, after all, given him an awful lot to ponder on. Finally he settled his penetrating eyes on mine. 'There can be no gainsaying that you and your men have done the Union Pacific a tremendous service by recovering the gold, but what proof have you got that Mister Dix is guilty of what you claim?'

Grabbing the Henry rifle from Elijah, I placed it on the desk. 'I took this from a dead Sioux warrior out on the plains. The white men that supplied them worked for Dix.'

'Except that, by your own testimony, they just all happen to be dead now,' that man sneered. 'You're just a cold-blooded killer, and the railroad has got no business employing you.'

'I'm still waiting for the proof, Mister Wakefield,' the chief engineer added patiently.

'Have you seen this before?' I asked, handing over the telegraph.

As he noted the addressee and then read the contents of Casement's message, Dodge's eyebrows rose in astonishment. 'No. No, I haven't.'

'I took it out of his pocket,' I responded. 'That's how he knew to send a trainload of hired guns after us, and why he was waiting at the depot when that same train returned. What it contained had to be for his eyes only.'

'That's preposterous,' Dix blustered. 'I just happened to be in the telegraph office when that message arrived, and as a director of this railroad I had every right to read it.'

Now, for the first time, Dodge regarded him dubiously. 'And so did I . . . since it just happened to be addressed to me, and me alone.' He paused slightly, before adding, 'All this can be checked, you know.'

Dix shook his head in apparent disbelief. 'There's nothing to check. After reading the telegraph, I sent some men to the railhead to escort the gold back here, and for some unaccountable reason these three lunatics apparently took against them. We can't confirm any of it, because the telegraph happens to be *conveniently* down. But in any case. . . .'

I'd had more than enough. 'I also have a witness to his bad deeds,' I interrupted loudly.

'Where?' Dodge demanded.

'Right here. Tell him, Elijah,' I instructed.

'A man working for Dix hired me to "do anything that's necessary", and that included roughing up the stablehand down at the livery, when we were searching for the men who'd recovered the gold. Thankfully, Joe redeemed me and showed me the error of my ways.'

'It's all absolute goddamned nonsense,' Dix protested. 'What possible reason would I have to employ a piece of gutter trash like this?'

Elijah reacted sharply by jabbing his boot into Dix's injured foot, eliciting a howl of pain.

'Enough of that!' Dodge barked, before returning his gaze to me. 'It's obvious to me that there have been certain irregularities; matters that need looking into. And there can be no refuting the fact that you have recovered all these Double Eagles. So, while I attempt to contact the railhead and make some sense of it all, I want you men to take Mister Dix to the saw-bones and get him patched up.'

I was mortified beyond belief. 'But ain't you gonna arrest him?'

Dodge shook his head in apparent bemusement. 'I'm no lawman, Mister Wakefield. I'm just building a railroad.'

'But this skunk has broken any number of laws. He deserves to pay, big style!'

'As far as I'm aware, there's no law against trading with Indians. The Comancheros in New Mexico have been doing it for decades. It is illegal by federal statute to sell them firearms, but unfortunately you have no real proof that Mister Dix has done that. As he inferred earlier, you have operated with *deadly* efficiency.'

'So he's just gonna limp off into the sunset then, is that it?' I asked bitterly. Then, suddenly it was all so clear, and before he could answer, I added, 'Oh, I see

152

what this is. He's a director. One of you, and you're looking out for him.'

Dodge's eyes narrowed slightly, and his lips appeared to tighten over his teeth. 'You three have done very well for the Union Pacific. You especially, Wakefield, could have a very good future with the railroad. Don't spoil it all now.' He paused before adding, 'I suggest that you get moving.'

Surprisingly, Dan was quick to react to the warning. Tugging at my sleeve, he said, 'Come on, Josiah, let's take this pus weasel off to the sawbones.'

Dix was horrified. 'You can't send me off with them. They're not fit to wipe my boots!'

For the first time, genuine anger flared on the chief engineer's face. 'I've heard a deal of unpleasant accusations about you, Oliver. I suggest you to leave me to think on them. If there has been serious bloodshed at the railhead, it may be that the board of directors will need to be notified. Time will tell. Go!'

Heaving Dix to his feet reluctantly, I frogmarched him out of the room and along the corridor. I was seething with anger, and would happily have kicked him down the stairs. But of course I couldn't do that. If he was to break his neck, I had little doubt that for the likes of me there would be no immunity from the law. This jumped-up diminutive shit, with his fancy duds and superior airs, was going to get away with his crimes, and there wasn't a damn thing I could do about it!

With my purloined LeMat made safe and tucked in

my belt, I reached the ornate lobby, completely ignoring the renewed stares of the various flunkeys. Anger was turning to dejection, to the extent that our recovery of the stolen payroll no longer seemed like much of an achievement.

'For a man that's done real good, you don't look too chipper,' Elijah remarked as he came level with me.

I grimaced. 'That ain't hardly surprising. And it ain't all down to this bull turd escaping justice. I've got to return to the railhead and apologise to Jack Casement. That's gonna be way harder than anything I've done all year!'

CHAPTER THIRTEEN

Gratefully escaping the confines of the hotel, I stepped down on to the dirt street, which in truth was where I felt I belonged. The meeting with Dodge could definitely have gone better. In fact, if it had continued much longer, it was quite possible that I might have talked myself out of a job. I still grasped the LeMat, and actually hoped that Dix might make a break for it. For a long moment I just stood there, breathing deeply, as though getting my bearings. Instinctively, the hurting railroad director seemed to realize that silence was his safest option.

With an influx of workers for first the telegraph and then the railroad, Omaha had long been known as a cesspool of lawlessness. But as usual, where there was an absence of law, there was often opportunity for enterprising medical practitioners. And, unsurprisingly considering our current mission, it was as though Dan had read my mind.

'No dearth of sawbones in this burg, Josiah,' he

commented. 'In fact I recall seeing a sign for one a short ways down here, on the left.'

'Happen you're spot on, Dan,' I replied with sudden warmth. It suddenly hit home that with friends around me, nothing else really mattered overmuch. Glancing scornfully at our patient, I tightened my grip on the collar of his frockcoat. 'Come on *Mister* Dix. Let's take us a little stroll down 9th Street.'

Omaha was a thriving city, and the thoroughfare teamed with pedestrians and horse-drawn vehicles of every kind. Consequently we formed a tight-nit group, as we slowly, and in Dix's case painfully, threaded our way towards our destination. Off to our left was a barbershop, followed by a dry goods store. After our gruelling trials and tribulations, it all appeared undeniably pleasant and normal. With the sun's rays warming my back, and the sights and sounds of everyday life around us, I began to feel a little perkier.

Almost in our midst, a gunshot crashed out, and warm liquid splashed onto the left-hand side of my face. Reactively, I glanced in that direction. Elijah's dark features were no longer recognizable, just bone and bloody pulp. Even as he began to crumple to the dirt, I caught sight of a small figure in the narrow alley between the two buildings.

'He's mine,' Dan bellowed, triggering his Spencer. 'Watch your back!'

Sound words indeed. As our unknown assailant grunted under the force of a heavy bullet striking his shoulder, I retained my grip on Dix and bodily swung his light frame ninety degrees to my right. Directly before us, a big man levelled his Colt Army revolver and fired. The ball slammed into my prisoner's chest, but thankfully did not exit through his back. With strength noticeably draining from his legs, I desperately kept hold of him and cocked my LeMat. As the hammer came back, I flicked up the small lever within it, so altering the striker mode.

With women screaming, and the street clearing rapidly, I peered over at my attacker. Only then did I recognize him. 'You!' I exclaimed.

The burly river pirate, whose right foot I had wrecked by the side of the Missouri, stood before me frantically searching for a target. 'Show yourself, you bastard!' he snarled.

Hunched over, and straining from the effort, I just managed to keep Dix's dying form upright. 'Dried your piece out, have you?' I sneered, antagonising him deliberately. More shots rang out behind me, but I could only ignore them and trust to Dan's ability.

The big bruiser attempted to outmanoeuvre me by shifting position rapidly, but his crippled foot badly let him down. Frustration began to affect his judgement, and he took another poorly judged shot at my human shield. As Dix's body absorbed another smashing blow, I swung my right arm out and levelled the LeMat. It was not my weapon, and so I could only trust that it had been loaded properly.

As I squeezed the trigger, there was a tremendous crash as the shotgun charge erupted from the stubby barrel of the over-and-under weapon. Because of my posture, the full load struck my opponent in his groin. The devastating blow instantaneously ended any further resistance. With an inhuman scream, he dropped to his knees, the Colt falling from his grasp. His tormented eyes settled on mine, although whether I now actually registered with him was debatable.

'I told you what I'd do if I ever saw you again,' I reminded him through bared teeth. 'Killing my friend only made that even more of a certainty.'

Although drenched with blood and twitching uncontrollably, he still managed to summon a belligerent response. 'Go to hell, you tarnal cockchafer!'

Allowing Dix's redundant cadaver to slip from my grasp, I placed the LeMat's muzzle mere inches from my victim's forehead and muttered, 'Very possibly, but you first.' That said, I squeezed the trigger again.

Even as the ball pierced his skull, flame from the flash seared his brutalised features. His shattered head jerked back and then rapidly forward, before his whole body collapsed irrevocably into the dust.

'He had some hard bark on him,' I remarked, knowing full well that since I was still alive, then so Dan must also be.

Anxiously turning around, I beheld a scene of pure carnage. Both Elijah and his stoop shouldered assailant were unquestionably dead. Dan was white-faced, but standing without support. His left arm hung loose, with blood dripping from his fingertips, but he still managed a wan smile as he saw my horrified expression.

'Don't trouble yourself, Josiah. It's a flesh wound, is all. Just a pure shame that the same ain't true of Elijah.'

I nodded bleakly. 'He might have strayed into bad ways for a time, but he sure didn't deserve this . . . unlike all these other sons of bitches!'

Dan indicated Dix's blood-soaked corpse. 'Looks like I'm gonna be taking his place at the sawbones. Dodge ain't gonna like this outcome a whole lot.'

I grunted. 'It is what it is. What you might call a turn of events, and one that he'll just have to accept. After all, he's got the company's gold back, the gunrunners are dead, and we even killed a few Sioux for him. That's got to be worth ten dollars a day and found.'

Dan eyes blinked rapidly, as though he was absorbing some unsettling information. '*How much?*'

'Oh, shit!'